MW00411804

Garden Girls
Cozy Mystery Series Book 10
Hope Callaghan

***

hopecallaghan.com

Visit my website for new releases and special offers: hopecallaghan.com

Thank you, Peggy Hyndman for taking the time to preview *Home for the Holidays,* for the extra sets of eyes and for catching all my mistakes.

TABLE OF CONTENTS

Chapter 1

"Oh, this isn't going to work." Gloria Rutherford stared into the floor mirror and squinted at her reflection. The dress was...well, not Gloria. It was too fluffy, too puffy and to be perfectly honest, it made her look too young.

Gloria did not want to appear "matronly." After all, this was to be her wedding dress. She wanted something that screamed "classy and elegant."

Dot, one of Gloria's close friends, tugged on a "poofy" sleeve and wrinkled her nose. "Yeah. I can see your point. I think I spotted one on the rack that might be more your style."

Dot didn't wait for a reply as she darted back inside the main showroom floor of the boutique store in search of the dress she deemed a better choice.

Lucy flopped into a cushioned chair situated next to the mirrors and leaned back. "This dress makes you look like a..."

"Cake topper," Ruth quipped.

Margaret clamped her hand over her mouth to hide her grin and nodded.

Gloria stepped off the raised platform and followed Dot. At this point, she was sick of trying on dresses. The dress she envisioned in her mind was akin to finding a needle in a haystack.

Dot met her halfway across the showroom floor. "I have three and will bet money you'll fall in love with at least one of these." She thrust the dresses into Gloria's outstretched arms, placed her hand on Gloria's back and guided her to the oversized dressing rooms in the rear of the shop.

"But..."

Dot shook her head firmly. "No buts. Now get in there and try them on!"

Gloria obediently tromped into the dressing room and closed the door. No wonder she dreaded dress shopping. The last time she had worn a wedding dress she had been eighteen years old.

Maybe she would be better off wearing a pantsuit instead. She reached for the door handle and paused. That wouldn't be fair to Paul. She could envision him waiting for her at the altar and the look on his face when she showed up wearing slacks.

Gloria tugged the dress up, reached over her shoulder and unzipped the back of the cake topper she was wearing. She studied all three dresses Dot had given her in an attempt to figure out which dress would work best.

She studied the first dress with a critical eye. Too plain. She set the dress aside and lifted the second one. She immediately dismissed it. The dress weighed at least ten pounds.

When she held up dress number three, she paused. It was elegant. The outer layer consisted of sheer material. The upper part of the dress was scalloped lace. The lace ended near the waistline. From the middle down, it was a layer of antique white lace covered by the same sheer, tulle material.

Strips of satin circled the middle. Small jewels decorated the neckline and quarter sleeves.

Gloria sucked in a breath and held the dress up. It was perfect. She unzipped the back and slipped it over her head. It fit like a glove, as if the dress had been made for her.

She reached behind and zipped the back halfway, as far as she could reach and then studied her reflection. The hem fell just below her knee.

Gloria smoothed a hand over the material. This was the dress!

Gloria opened the dressing room door and peeked around the corner. Six sets of expectant eyes stared back: Lucy, Ruth, Margaret, Dot, Andrea and Alice.

"Well?" Lucy asked.

Gloria pushed the door wide open and stepped into the room.

The girls gasped.

"It's perfect!" Lucy exclaimed.

"You look like a million bucks," Ruth said.

Alice clapped her hands. "Mr. Paul is a lucky man."

Andrea nodded her approval. "It fits you perfectly."

Dot circled Gloria and stopped in the back to finish zipping the dress. "See? I told you!"

Gloria beamed. "I love it."

"So will Paul," Lucy predicted.

The sales clerk rounded the corner and studied the dress critically. "It is a perfect fit. You won't need alterations."

"Great!" Gloria said. "I'll take it with me."

The sales clerk carefully arranged the dress on a silk hangar and then slipped a clear, plastic bag over the top. Gloria stopped near the shoe rack on her way to the cash register where she found a matching pair of shoes and slip that would work perfect.

Gloria paid for her purchases and grabbed her goodies. "One stop shopping. Just my style."

The girls all piled into Ruth's van. Ruth glanced in the rearview mirror. "Now where?"

"Lunch," Gloria said. "I picked out the perfect place." Today was a special day and Gloria planned to treat her best friends to a special lunch. It was a rare occasion when they all got together for a shopping trip, especially Andrea and Alice, and Gloria wanted to make it a day they wouldn't soon forget.

Their destination was a brand new seafood restaurant in Grand Rapids, situated on the banks of the Grand River. So far, the upscale restaurant had gotten rave reviews.

Gloria had passed by the place not long ago. She directed Ruth to the restaurant. Ruth pulled into the drive and parked in an empty spot. She shut the engine off and peered out the front window. "This place looks swanky."

"Don't worry about it," Gloria told her friend. "Lunch is on me."

Gloria had called ahead and the staff assured her they would reserve a private table with a view of the river. The girls crowded into the lobby and the hostess led them to the table.

When they reached the table, Gloria nodded her approval. It was perfect and the view of the river breathtaking.

After they ordered drinks, all eyes turned to Alice. "How is the *At Your Service* Dog Services coming along?" Lucy asked.

Alice grinned. "Oh. It is going good. You should come visit. It will be next year before any of the dogs are ready for new homes but we have started training."

Gloria lifted her water glass and sipped from the straw. "What about the kennel?" In addition to training the dogs as service dogs, they were adding a boarding kennel, designed to keep money flowing in.

Alice reached for her napkin, unfolded the silverware and placed the napkin in her lap. "Yes. We have several bookings for the holidays and more calls are coming in every day. Plus, we have found homes for many of the dogs who are older or cannot be trained."

The food arrived and the conversation paused. Gloria had ordered the coconut macadamia shrimp. The server shifted the plate from the tray and placed it in front of her. He positioned the plate so the shrimp was front and center.

The pieces of shrimp were large and arranged over a heaping bed of rice and vegetables. Her mouth watered as she sliced off a large piece of shrimp, dipped it in the sauce and popped it in her mouth.

7

Gloria had chosen a creamy lemon cocktail sauce. The tart from the lemon and the mixture of cream cheese and sour cream was the perfect combination. It was melt in your mouth with a hint of pucker. She savored the flavors and reached for a scoop of rice.

The other girls ranted and raved over their dishes and Gloria was glad she had chosen the restaurant for the special occasion.

After they finished a long, leisurely meal, they decided to stop at Enchanting Petals, a floral shop in Green Springs, on their way home.

Picking out flowers was one of the last items on Gloria's to-do list. She already had a mental image of what she wanted – a winter-themed ensemble.

The girls crowded inside the small store. Gloria scanned the various arrangements on display and easily decided on a bouquet of winter white roses with sprigs of cranberry and holly tucked in. A layer of twigs formed the base of the bouquet. A shimmering silver ribbon tied around the lower section held the arrangement together.

For the dinner tables, the girls decided on classy, yet simple and stumbled upon round pillar candles with sprigs of eucalyptus circling the outside. A silky, cream-colored ribbon held the eucalyptus in place.

After Gloria finished picking out the arrangements and scheduling the delivery, the girls headed back to the van.

The day had been a huge success and Gloria was thrilled she could mark one more chore off her wedding list.

Ruth pulled into her drive and the girls hopped out of the van. She made her way 'round back, opened the van's rear cargo door and reached for Gloria's dress. "Hang it up right away so it doesn't wrinkle," she said.

Gloria took the bag and scrunched her nose. "I hope it's not too late," she fretted.

Dot grabbed the shopping bag that held the shoes and slip. "Don't forget the other goodies."

Gloria reached for the bag. "Thanks." She had been forgetful lately. There seemed to be so much to do and she was running out of time. She had made a list and faithfully checked off things as she went along. Despite that, she was still feeling overwhelmed.

In addition to the wedding, Gloria's two sons and their families would be arriving soon and she would have a house full of people. There were family get-togethers planned, rehearsal dinner, decorating Andrea's beautiful home for the wedding. The list went on and on.

On top off all that, Paul was retiring. His last day as a sheriff at Montbay County Sheriff Department was next week and a large retirement party had been planned. Gloria was nervous. Paul was nervous. Heck, even Gloria's dog, Mally, was nervous. At least she had been acting that way.

She placed her precious treasures in the trunk of the car before she made her rounds, hugging each of her dear friends and thanking them for making the day a memorable one.

Gloria followed Lucy out of Ruth's drive and headed home. When she pulled into her own drive, she was surprised to see Paul's truck parked next to the garage. He had told her the day before they had switched shifts on him and asked him to work the next few days instead of the night shift.

Gloria parked Annabelle in front of the drive, climbed out of the driver's seat and opened the trunk. She grabbed the hook of the hangar, carefully balancing it in one hand as she reached for the shoes and the slip.

Gloria folded the clear, plastic cover in half and hoped Paul wouldn't get even a glimpse of the dress she had picked out.

She climbed the porch steps and shifted her treasures as she reached for the doorknob.

Paul pulled the door open as she reached for the knob. He leaned forward in an attempt to take something from his bride-to-be's overflowing arms. "Let me help!"

Gloria handed him the shoes and slip but held firmly to the dress. "No can do. I'll keep this."

She didn't stop in the kitchen, but rather headed straight to the bedroom in the back. She closed the bedroom door, stepped over to the closet and turned on the closet light as she peered at her dress.

A smile lit her face as she turned the dress around. She loved the dress even more than she remembered. It was perfect!

The boutique clerk had included a deluxe padded hanger and Gloria slipped the ends under the shoulders. She opened her closet door and hung the dress in the special spot she had cleared out in anticipation of the dress.

Gloria closed the door and made her way back into the kitchen.

Paul was sitting at the table, staring out the window. Gloria could tell from the look on his face he was a million miles away. She stepped over to the kitchen sink, squirted a glob of soap in her hands and turned the knobs on. "I thought you had to work today."

"Huh?" Paul turned with a blank expression covering his face.

Gloria scrubbed her hands, turned the water off and reached for the hand towel to dry them.

Gloria hung the towel on the oven handle before turning to give Paul her full attention. Something was wrong...

"I thought you were at work," she said.

Paul dropped his hands into his lap and clasped them together. "Captain Davies called me into his office first thing this morning."

Paul shifted in his chair and gazed at Gloria. "It seems while cleaning out my locker, some items were found..." His voice trailed off.

Gloria held her breath. Whatever was coming next was not going to be good.

"I'm under investigation for extortion."

Chapter 2

"How..." Gloria's thoughts went in a million different directions. "Extortion? Like in blackmailing someone?"

Paul nodded. "It seems someone tipped the captain off that I had bundles of cash stashed inside my locker. When he investigated yesterday, they found a duffel bag loaded with money."

He went on. "On top of the cash was an envelope and inside the envelope were two notes. The first note was addressed to Mitzi Verona and the other to City Commissioner Cal Evergreen."

Gloria's eyes widened. Cal Evergreen's face and name was all over the local news recently. He had been involved with a well-known "lady of the night," Pandora Gillette.

Mitzi Verona was a local celebrity. She came from a family of wealthy developers. Her father had helped build many of the downtown Grand Rapids office buildings. Mitzi's sons had recently taken over the day-to-day operations of the business.

There had been recent rumors of a division amongst the family members and Mitzi, the matriarch of the family, had been drawn into the family feud when an unknown source leaked to the press that some members of the family were involved in illegal online gambling.

"They think you were blackmailing these people and that's where the piles of cash came from?"

Paul ran a ragged hand across his crew cut. "I can't go into detail other than to say someone is trying to hang me with this."

Paul tilted his head and looked squarely into Gloria's eyes. "Can you believe it? Less than two weeks from retiring and now, I'm under investigation."

He shook his head. "If they decide to press charges, not only will I lose all of my benefits and my pension, I could end up in prison."

The color drained from Gloria's face. How could this be? Why would someone do this to Paul?

Gloria slid into the chair next to him, propped her elbows on the table and dropped her chin into her open palm. She fixed her gaze on his solemn face. "It's obviously someone who has access to the locker room. Maybe it was a co-worker...a fellow officer."

Paul's shoulders sagged. "We may have to postpone the wedding until I can get this sorted out. I don't want you saddled with a convicted criminal."

Gloria's mouth went dry. She stiffened her back and stared at him in disbelief. "You're kidding."

Paul slowly rose from the chair as he shook his head. "No. I'm sorry, but I need to get to the bottom of this and clear my name."

Gloria stared at him, her mouth gaping open as he slid his arms into his jacket and made his way to the porch door.

"There's more to the story, Gloria, but I can't tell you right now. I think it's best if we take a step back." Paul stopped short of calling off the wedding, but Gloria knew that was what he meant.

Paul opened the door. "I need be alone." He slowly closed the door behind him and shuffled to his truck.

Gloria, in a state of shock, walked over to the kitchen window and looked out. She watched Paul back out of her drive and wondered if this would be the last time she would ever see him again.

***

Gloria stared out the window with hollow eyes. It felt as if someone had punched her in the gut. Had she imagined Paul in her kitchen? The whole thing seemed surreal.

Mally nudged Gloria's hand and let out a low whine, pulling Gloria from her state of disbelief. She absentmindedly patted her head. "L-let's go out for a walk." It was late afternoon and soon it would be dark, too dark to visit her favorite spot in the woods.

Gloria grabbed her jacket, slipped it on and then opened the door. While Mally galloped out into the back of the yard, Gloria made a pit stop inside the garage to grab a flashlight.

Mally darted back and forth waiting for Gloria to catch up, unaware that Gloria's world had crumbled around her.

What if Paul fabricated the story because he had a case of cold feet and he didn't know how to tell Gloria he didn't want to marry her after all?

Had he suddenly decided she was too much to handle? Sure, she had been in a few tight spots ever since they started dating, but he was well aware of her penchant for snooping around and getting into some real humdinger situations. In fact, that was how they met.

Her heart froze at the last thought that popped into her head. Had Paul met someone else? She would be heartbroken! Gloria would be the laughingstock of Belhaven, left at the altar. She would have to leave town, move to Florida where her sister, Liz, lived.

Mally and Gloria reached the edge of the woods - "Gloria's woods." While Mally darted off to inspect the creek, Gloria made her way over to her favorite resting spot, the old log tree not far from the creek.

Tears welled up in her eyes when she reached the downed tree. The tree had splintered in two, the pieces separated by a narrow gap...just like Gloria's heart. She eased onto one side of the splintered log and stared sightlessly at Mally.

A tear trickled down her cheek and splashed onto her hand. Her world had shattered and she didn't know what to do.

Gloria's children would be arriving soon. She was supposed to walk down the aisle, to marry the man she loved. Now, she would have to call the flower shop, call Andrea and Dot and let them know they wouldn't need the mountains of food they had bought.

Gloria's three grandsons had been thrilled about being in Gram's wedding. How could she tell Ryan, Tyler and Ollie there would be no wedding? Not to mention her granddaughter, Ariel, who was to be Gloria's flower girl.

A sob caught in the back of Gloria's throat and the dam of tears spilled out as Gloria sobbed as she had the day they placed her husband, James, in the ground.

She lowered her head into her hands and anguished cries rocked her body. She bawled until her stomach pinched and her heart ached.

Mally darted over and nudged her nose between Gloria's hands in an attempt to comfort her.

Gloria wrapped her arms around Mally's neck and placed her cheek against her fur.

Finally, the flow of tears ended. Gloria wiped the back of her hand across her wet face and struggled to her feet. "It's time to go home," she said. "Alone."

Shadows from the evening sky hovered over the tree line as the two of them wandered out of the woods and into the open field.

A snowflake floated down and touched the tip of Gloria's nose. She stared up at the skies. Weather forecasters had predicted a long, snowy winter and in fact, they were supposed to get several inches of snow overnight.

The skies opened up and heavy, wet snowflakes began to fall. It was as if Gloria had stepped inside a snow globe.

She tugged at the edge of her coat and pulled the zipper a little higher. She hadn't bothered with a scarf or hat and by the time she reached the edge of the yard, her head was covered in a halo of white.

A coat of white covered Mally, too. The two of them stopped at the bottom of the steps leading to the porch. Mally shook her body, pelting Gloria and the steps with clumps of wet snow.

Mally scampered up the steps and waited on the porch while Gloria stomped her feet on the rug and unlocked the kitchen door.

Puddles, Gloria's cat, was sprawled out on the kitchen floor. He opened one eye and peered at them.

Mally trotted over to Puddles and greeted her pal with droplets of melted snow. Puddles was not a fan of the water. He scrambled upright and dashed out of the kitchen.

Despite her heavy heart, the exchange caused Gloria to grin. She pulled her cell phone from her jacket pocket and glanced at the screen. Lucy had called.

Gloria pressed the button on the front of the screen, tapped in the access code and listened to the message.

"Hi Gloria. It's me. Lucy. I-uh. Well. I was watching the six o'clock news..."

Gloria squeezed her eyes shut. She could tell by the tone in Lucy's voice that somehow Paul's investigation was on the evening news. Which meant everyone knew...

Lucy was still talking. "Yeah. Uh. Give me a call when you get this message. Bye."

Gloria had no intention of calling Lucy or anyone else for that matter. At least not right now. What had started out as a wonderful day had become a nightmare.

Paul was under investigation. The wedding was off. The whole Town of Belhaven probably watched the news. The only thing they didn't know was the wedding was off.

She shrugged out of her damp coat and hung it on the hook by the door. She slipped off her boots and set them in the boot tray.

It was dinnertime and Gloria wasn't hungry. She fed Mally and Puddles and then shut off the kitchen light.

The blinking light of the answering machine caught her eye. She had messages and could only imagine all of her friends - and family had heard the news.

Her stomach churned at the thought of explaining the situation. Tomorrow was another day. She didn't have the heart or willpower to talk to anyone tonight.

Gloria walked into the living room and switched on the lamp near her recliner. She had recently rearranged her living room furniture in preparation for the onslaught of family that would soon descend on her. It was the first time she had changed the furniture around since James' death. The new arrangement made the living room look even larger.

Tyler and Ryan had come over the previous weekend and helped Gloria put up the Christmas tree and other decorations. She fleetingly thought about turning the tree lights on but was too depressed.

She had recently purchased a second recliner to match her own so Paul and she could sit side-by-side and watch TV together.

Tears burned the back of her eyes as she gazed longingly at "his" empty recliner.

She eased into her chair and flipped the lever on the side. She had settled in for a full-blown pity party when she heard a knock on the back door.

"Go away," she moaned, although she was certain whoever was on the other side of the house couldn't possibly have heard.

Moments later, the knock came again. This time it was louder...much louder.

"Go away!" she shouted.

The third time was all out pounding and Gloria knew whoever was banging on the door had no intention of leaving.

She shoved the chair into the upright position, stomped to the kitchen, flipped the light and peeked through the blinds.

A freckled face, surrounded by bright red hair peered back at her. It was Lucy.

She shook her head, "no" but Lucy was not going to take no for an answer. She stubbornly crossed her arms and met Gloria's gaze.

Gloria sucked in a breath and swung the door open. "Misery doesn't like company," she blurted out.

Lucy barged past her friend and stepped into the kitchen. "Hiding out in your house isn't going to help."

Gloria pulled out a kitchen chair and sank down. "It isn't going to hurt either."

Lucy eased into the chair across from her. "Did you see the news?"

Gloria glumly shook her head. "Nope. No need. Paul was waiting for me when I got home. He told me what happened."

Lucy drummed her fingers on the kitchen table. "Someone is obviously trying to pin this on him."

Gloria lowered her chin and closed her eyes. "Yep."

"I think he's going to call off wedding. I'm moving to Florida," she blurted out. She hadn't actually decided until that precise moment, that was her plan. It seemed like a good one, though. Although living near Liz wasn't a rational decision. Gloria wasn't thinking clearly.

Lucy shot up out of her seat. "He is? You are?"

"No sense in sticking around here. I'll be the object of everyone's pity. 'There's poor Gloria. Left at the altar by a crooked cop.'"

Gloria's shoulders slumped. "I can hear it now."

"So you're going to duck and run." Lucy tsk-tsked. "Gloria Rutherford, I never pegged you as a quitter."

Maybe Gloria was a quitter. Maybe she was tired. Maybe both.

"I..." Gloria was about to reply when a tap on the door interrupted her. "Let me guess." She slid out of the chair, walked over to the window and lifted the corner of the blind.

This time, instead of one set of eyes staring back at her, there were multiple sets of eyes. Too many to count.

"I might as well let them in," Gloria grumbled and reached for the door handle.

She opened the door and stepped to the side. In walked Margaret, Dot, Ruth and Andrea.

"Hail, hail. The gang is all here." Gloria muttered.

Margaret didn't wait for an invitation as she dragged a chair from the table, plopped down and dropped her purse on the floor. "If you would answer your phone, maybe we wouldn't show up unannounced," she grumbled.

"Actually, we did announce it," Dot pointed out. "We left a message telling Gloria if she didn't call back, we were coming over."

Gloria rubbed her brow. "I'm too depressed to talk."

"No problem," Ruth said. "We'll do the talking." She turned to Lucy. "She knows."

Lucy slowly nodded. "Yeah. Gloria has some news."

All eyes turned to Gloria.

"The wedding is off. I'm moving to Florida."

Chapter 3

The room erupted in total chaos as six voices fought to be heard over the others.

Gloria tried to get a word in, but the chatter was so loud, no one was listening. Finally, she jumped out of the chair and held up her hands. "Girls!"

The room grew silent and five pairs of eyes lifted. "I appreciate you all coming here and showing moral support but my heart is broken. I don't even know how to begin to pick up the pieces."

She went on. "On top of all that, how can I show my face around town, knowing that people are whispering about me behind my back?"

Lucy spoke first. "So you're going to hightail it and run to Florida? To be with Liz of all people!"

It did sound crazy to Gloria, even in her altered state of mind. Living near Liz would be like living next to an insane asylum!

Lucy could see it was sinking in. Gloria wasn't in a state of mind to make major life decisions, namely moving halfway across the country.

Gloria shook her head and slumped back down in the chair. "What else can I do?" she answered in a small voice. "Paul all but came out and said it was over."

Dot, the voice of reason, spoke. "He's in the same state of shock you are. Neither one of you should be making decisions right now."

Dot's words rang true. Of course, Paul was in shock. She was in shock. Their lives had been turned upside down. "I don't know what to do."

Andrea piped up. "As a very dear, very close friend likes to tell me all the time, right before she drags me into one of her escapades, 'It's time to get to the bottom of this.'"

Gloria grinned despite the seriousness of her situation. Andrea was right. Dot was right. They were all right. She lifted her eyes and shifted her gaze as she looked at each of her friends. "I need your help."

Margaret rolled her eyes. "That is why we're here, silly!"

Ruth rubbed her hands together. "We need to come up with a plan."

Dot frowned. "This might be a tough one. How do we gain access to the inside of the police department to snoop around?"

"We should talk to Paul first," Andrea suggested. She glanced at Gloria's clock above the kitchen sink. It was already 8:30 at night. "How about first thing in the morning?"

They agreed that overwhelming him with all of them at once might be a bad idea. Instead, they decided to send Lucy and Margaret.

"What should I do?" Gloria asked.

She had a sudden thought. "There is a cop hangout in Green Springs. It's a 24-hour diner popular with police, especially the ones who work the night shift." Paul's shift.

Andrea snapped her fingers. "Great! Why don't we run by there?" She turned to Gloria. "I'm a night owl and I doubt you'll get any sleep."

It was true. The night loomed long and lonely.

She pressed on. "We need to get this investigation started. There's a wedding right around the corner!"

Gloria wasn't convinced. There was still a little voice whispering in her ear that maybe, just maybe, Paul was trying to get out of marrying her. Her pride wouldn't admit it...at least not out loud, but the terrible little voice was echoing the words, no matter how hard she tried to push them out.

"Okay," she relented. "You're right. I won't sleep a wink tonight."

The girls abandoned the chairs and headed for the door.

"I'll keep my ears open," Ruth promised.

"Me, too." Dot added.

"What time should we show up on Paul's doorstep in the morning?" Margaret asked.

Gloria guessed if Paul were in the same state of mind she was, he wouldn't sleep well and would be up early. She shrugged her shoulders. "Whenever you want. I'm not sure how cooperative he'll be," she admitted.

Lucy patted Gloria's shoulder. "Don't worry about Paul. We'll figure something out."

It was a good thing they were. Gloria's mind was still a pile of mush and she was having trouble forming a coherent thought.

Gloria was the last one out of the kitchen. She slid her arms in her coat, grabbed her keys and then pulled the back door shut. She wiggled the knob to make sure it had locked.

Andrea offered to drive and Gloria was relieved. She hated driving at night. It was hard for her to judge distance after dark. On top of that, she was still distraught over the day's turn of events.

She hugged each of her friends before she climbed into the passenger seat of Andrea's pick-up. She reached for the seatbelt, slid it across her lap and clicked the latch into the buckle.

Andrea fastened her own seat belt and turned the key in the ignition. "Don't worry, Gloria. We will get to the bottom of this. I promise," she vowed.

Gloria nodded. Sudden tears burned the back of her eyes. Her friends...and family were the most important things in the world. There was no way she could leave Belhaven. This was the only home she had ever known.

Talk of moving to Florida was Gloria in panic-mode. She was starting to calm down and rational thoughts returned.

Her mind kicked into detective gear as she tried to remember some of the people Paul worked with. She had met several of them during the past summer when Paul's boss, Captain Davies, had hosted a cookout at his cabin on the shores of Crooked Pine Lake.

She closed her eyes and leaned her head against the headrest. "Paul and I went to a cookout last summer with some of his co-workers, fellow officers. I'm trying to remember their names."

Several of the officers were close to Paul's age...close to retirement age. She was terrible with names and gave up trying to remember them. Instead, Gloria focused on the details.

There was a short, balding guy who teased Paul that he was about a year behind him in retirement. He had mentioned his wife was hounding him to buy an RV so they could travel around the country. Stan something...

Then there were two brothers. They were still in their 30's if Gloria had to guess. The only reason she remembered them is they seemed standoffish when Gloria tried to make conversation.

There was one more person who stuck out. It was a rookie cop. He was 100% gung ho, by the book, a stickler for rules, spouting off his list of accomplishments. He rubbed Gloria the wrong way when he told her he was glad Paul was retiring, that there needed to be a "changing of the guard" as he put it. Gloria did remember his name. It was Alex and the only reason she remembered was she thought his name should have been Alec, as in smart aleck.

Andrea pulled the truck into the diner parking lot. The place was hopping at nine o'clock at night. The majority of the vehicles were police cruisers. Gloria wondered how many times a week Paul had dropped by to talk to his fellow officers and grab a bite to eat.

Andrea led the way inside and Gloria trailed behind. The sign just inside the door told them to seat themselves, which Andrea promptly did...right in the middle of the area filled with cops.

Other restaurant patrons chose the other side of the restaurant but not Andrea. Of course, that was the whole reason they were there. To see if they could glean any information, eavesdrop on conversations, maybe chat with the waitress.

Gloria quickly studied the faces before taking a seat in the booth across from Andrea. She reached for the menu and opened the front flap as she pretended to peruse the menu items. She had skipped dinner and realized the last time she had eaten was at the fancy seafood restaurant earlier in the day with the girls.

It seemed so long ago now...like an eternity, not a few short hours.

Her stomach grumbled as she read the breakfast items. This was definitely a bacon and eggs kind of night. The waitress arrived with two cups of coffee. She jotted the girls' orders on her notepad and slipped it inside her apron.

"I'll get right on this," she said.

Andrea thanked the girl and then leaned back in an attempt to eavesdrop on the officers seated at the booth directly behind them. She tilted her blonde head.

"...then when I turned around, he was face first in the toilet bowl, gulping yellow water."

She snapped her head upright and looked at Gloria. "Too gross. Let's move." Her eyes scanned the room. She spotted another empty booth, right next to a booth with three officers.

She scrambled out of the seat and Gloria followed behind. The table had been cleared but not cleaned.

Gloria reached inside her purse, pulled out a clean tissue and swiped at the crumbs on the table.

The waitress darted over when she noticed Gloria cleaning. "You moved."

Andrea scrunched her nose and nodded. "Yeah. Uh, the conversation next to us was not conducive to eating, you could say."

The waitress leaned forward and took over for Gloria as she wiped the table with a clean, wet rag.

"Yeah. They have some doozy conversations. Guess it goes with the territory."

When she finished wiping, she whirled around and made her way back behind the diner counter.

Andrea picked up the menu and focused her attention on the table behind her. This time, she hit the jackpot.

"...is gunning for his job, anyway. Nice, cushy office and all. Seems like those rumors swirling around for months now were true."

"You think Diane is gonna try and pull some strings to get this thing buried under the rug?" the cop on the other side asked.

The officer across from him shrugged. "Stone has been after Kennedy for months now. Who knows? Maybe he'll be willing to scratch her back if she scratches his."

The officer snickered and then changed the subject as they began to discuss a recent football game.

Andrea prayed Gloria hadn't overheard the part about the Diane woman but she had.

The muscle in Gloria's jaw twitched as she fought the urge to jump out of her seat, stomp over to the other booth and demand to know who Diane Stone was. "*Who* is Diane Stone?" she hissed as she leaned forward.

"This is hearsay," Andrea attempted to calm Gloria, whose face was a mask of fury. Her poor friend had had to endure every kind emotion. Joy, heartbreak, pain, fury...all in the same day.

Gloria reached for her phone. "Maybe it's time to find out."

Andrea reached across the table and put her hand on Gloria's arm. "I know you're angry and hurt. Paul may be completely innocent. It sounds like he turned this woman down," she pointed out.

Gloria let her cell phone drop back inside her purse. "True. It did sound that way."

Andrea pressed on. "You have had a long day. He has had a long day. Why don't you sleep on this before you call him up and give him the third degree?"

Andrea's voice of reason won out. Gloria nodded. "Okay," she relented.

Their food arrived minutes later. The girls bowed their heads in prayer and Andrea prayed for peace and a quick solving of the mystery before she finished with "Amen."

Gloria lifted her napkin, placed it in her lap and reached for the shaker of salt. The smell of fried bacon wafted in the air and Gloria's mouth watered. She was starving.

Andrea kept to the safe subject of the upcoming visit from Gloria's sons, whom Andrea had never met but felt as if she already knew. "What time are the boys and family coming in?"

Gloria paused, her fork mid-air. Her brow formed a "v" and her mind drew a blank. "I-I don't remember." She shook her head to clear the fog. "Early afternoon...I think."

The officers behind Andrea slid out of the booth, dropped some bills on the table and headed toward the exit.

Andrea glanced around. The diner was almost empty.

The waitress returned with a fresh pot of coffee. "More coffee?"

Gloria covered her cup and shook her head. "No thanks." Coffee kept her awake, if she drank too much, although she knew she wouldn't get a wink of sleep tonight, anyway. She glanced at the nametag, *Ashley*. "Have you worked here long?"

Ashley nodded. "Yeah. Almost a year now." She balanced the pot of coffee on the edge of the table. "I'm working my way through college." She shrugged. "The tips are good, especially from the cops. They like to hang out and they drink a ton of coffee."

Andrea nodded. "I bet they do. You probably know quite a few of them."

"Yep. Most of 'em are good guys. There are a couple stinkers, though." Ashley wrinkled her nose.

Gloria was curious. "Stinkers as in stingy with their tips?" That would be her guess.

Ashley waved a hand. "No. More like rude. Like snappy. Maybe they're tired of the night shift, like me."

That could be true. Gloria knew she got cranky when she didn't get a good night's rest. "Do you have a favorite?"

"Yep. Officer Kennedy."

Gloria's heart leapt in her chest.

Ashley shook her head. "Such a shame he got into trouble. Not that I believe it. He was always full of kind words, encouraging me to hang in there and finish college."

She went on. "The other cops, they don't believe it either. Except for Jason Endres. He was in here talking smack earlier. Said he was sure Officer Kennedy was guilty as all get out."

Ashley placed her hand on her hip. "He's such a creep...always bragging about single-handedly taking down thugs. He patrolled with Officer Kennedy. Officer Kennedy must have the patience of a saint."

Gloria knew most of the time Paul patrolled alone, but there were times the officers patrolled in pairs. It depended on whether it was a holiday or special event where they needed more hands on deck.

After Ashley left, Gloria fumbled in her purse for her wallet. She left enough money to pay for both of their meals, over Andrea's protests. She also left an extra ten because kids could always use extra cash. She admired the young woman for juggling work and school and she prayed a quick prayer Ashley would stick with it until she graduated from college.

The girls exited the diner and climbed back inside the truck. It was after eleven by the time Andrea pulled into Gloria's drive. She shifted into park and turned to Gloria. "You want me to come in?"

Gloria reached for the handle and shook her head. "No. I'm feeling better now. I guess I was in shock."

"So if I come back in the morning, you won't have packed your bags and hit the road for Florida?" Andrea teased.

"Ha! No. What was I thinking?" Gloria twirled her finger in a circular motion near her head. She opened the truck door and stepped onto the ground. "Maybe I'll wait a couple days 'til the dust settles before I mention anything about moving or postponing the wedding."

"Good idea," Andrea agreed. "A lot can happen in a couple days. Who knows? Maybe by then we will have tracked down the person who set Paul up."

It was true. There was a chance that could happen. A slight chance...

Gloria crept up the steps and shuffled to the door. She fumbled with the keys and finally managed to unlock the door. She stepped inside and waved to Andrea, who waited until she was safely inside.

Gloria closed and locked the door. She leaned against the door and rested the back of her head against the glass pane.

Gloria was never so happy to see a day end.

Chapter 4

Gloria awoke abruptly. Her eyes flew open and she turned her head to peer at the clock on her nightstand. It was still early...and dark. Her eyes squinted as she focused on the blue light. It was 5:45 a.m.

Gloria fell back into bed, pulled the covers over her head and willed the sweet escape of sleep to return. Her body was on board, but her mind had already shifted into overdrive.

Finally, she gave up trying to sleep, flung the covers back and swung her legs over the side of the bed.

Mally whined from her doggy bed and shifted as she fell back asleep.

Gloria opened the bedroom door and crept into the living room.

The wind howled loudly and she could hear the screech of the tree branches as they scraped against the large picture window that faced the road.

It looked as if today would match Gloria's mood...dark and stormy.

Gloria switched on the living room lamp and crossed over into the dining room on her way to the kitchen.

She started a pot of coffee, turned on the porch light, opened the kitchen blinds and settled in at the kitchen table. A layer of snow covered the porch rail. The porch rail was Gloria's "unofficial" gauge of snowfall and this one looked to be about two inches worth.

The coffee had finished brewing and Gloria stepped over to the cupboard, pulled a coffee mug from the shelf and filled the mug before returning to the table.

She reached for her well-worn Bible and flipped it open to the spot she had marked. She searched in vain for words of comfort but the solace she sought eluded her.

Gloria flipped to the concordance in the back of her Bible and searched for "heartbroken."

She turned to the book of Proverbs and smiled as she read Proverbs 21, Verse 19:

"It is better to dwell in the wilderness, than with a contentious and angry woman." KJV.

Finally, she stumbled on a verse:

"My flesh and my heart faileth: but God is the strength of my heart, and my portion forever." Psalm 73:26 KJV

Gloria closed her eyes and bowed her head. "Lord, please help me make it through this." It was a simple, heartfelt prayer and said it all.

Mally dashed into the kitchen and came to a screeching halt at the back door. Gloria recognized the look on her face. She needed to go out.

She scrambled out of the chair and scooted over to the door. Gloria opened it wide and Mally darted out. Gloria's beloved pooch paused at the top of the stairs and stared out at the fresh blanket of snow covering the steps and as far as the eye could see. She put one paw on the snowy step and then lifted it back up.

Necessity won out and Mally bounded down the steps and into the yard.

Gloria grabbed her coat, slipped her arms in the sleeves and stepped onto the porch. The wind had died down and the snowfall had turned into light flurries.

The cold winter air nipped at Gloria's nose and made her feel alive. She was thankful for all of the blessings in her life, including Paul. God had brought the two of them together and yes, it seemed they had hit a bump in the road, but that was to be expected.

Gloria stiffened her back and resolved she...and her friends...would figure out who was trying to pin this extortion mess on Paul!

Gloria cupped her hands to her mouth. "C'mon, Mally! We have work to do!"

The two stepped back inside the warm, cozy kitchen and Gloria shut the door behind them. It was time to get down to business!

***

Gloria briefly remembered Margaret and Lucy telling her they were going to talk to Paul this morning to see if he had any idea who might be setting him up. She had a sneaking suspicion they were going to try to talk some sense into him about possibly postponing the wedding, too.

She was torn. On the one hand, she didn't want to have to convince someone to marry her. She had her pride, after all.

On the other hand, she thought he was punishing himself for something he had no control over. There was only one way to muddle through this mess and it was time for Gloria to hop back in the saddle, roll up her sleeves and start the investigation.

She popped two slices of bread in the toaster. After they toasted, she spread a layer of creamy peanut butter on one slice and placed it in Mally's food dish.

She put peanut butter and jelly on top of hers, folded it in half and munched on it as she settled in front of the computer.

Gloria grabbed a pen, a small notepad and jotted down the names of people she considered suspects. There was Alex, or as Gloria had nicknamed him, "Smart Aleck." He was the rookie who occasionally patrolled with Paul. Next was Jason Endres, another young hotshot cop. He was the one Andrea and she overhead was gunning for Paul's job.

Then there was Diane Stone. Gloria frowned as she added her name to the list. Was she a spurned woman, intent on punishing Paul? She remembered the saying, "Hell hath no fury like a woman scorned."

She tapped her pen on top of the pad. The woman may have motive, but where was the opportunity to place the cash and notes in Paul's locker? Gloria had never been inside the employee-only areas of the station but had to guess the women's locker room and the men's locker room were in separate areas.

Diane Stone would have to be gutsy to sneak into the men's locker room, if, in fact, she had even done it. Maybe she had an accomplice.

If only she could find a way to get into the police station to look around...but how? Sneaking into a police station would be like trying to break into Fort Knox. Perhaps she could recruit another officer, plead her case and appeal to his or her sense of justice. Maybe...

Gloria chewed her lower lip. Whom could she ask? The only person she trusted was Paul. There was no way he would allow her to get involved. In fact, she knew he would be upset if he had even an inkling she was nosing around.

Gloria abruptly rose from the chair and grabbed her empty coffee cup. She poured another cup and wandered over to the window. The sun was out and almost all of the pristine snow had melted, leaving behind a muddy mess.

She needed to get the driveway paved. The gravel helped keep the drive from turning into a soup bowl but it had been a couple years since she had more gravel brought in.

Maybe she should move to Florida. Gloria shook her head to clear the irrational thought and sipped her coffee.

Her eyes drifted to the road out front. She watched as Kenny, Belhaven Post Office's rural route carrier, zipped by in his mail truck. Right behind Kenny was Officer Joe Nelson's police cruiser.

Gloria's eyes grew wide. Officer Joe Nelson! Gloria had her mole!

Chapter 5

Officer Joe Nelson was a creature of habit and one of his habits was to stop by Dot's every morning at 7:30 a.m. on the dot for coffee (black), an egg white omelet, which consisted of two tablespoons sharp cheddar cheese, a handful of onion, bacon and green peppers...and two slices of whole wheat toast, no butter.

Dot had teased him for years that she knew he would either have to be dead or deathly ill to miss his morning ritual.

Gloria rushed to the bathroom, showered so fast the mirror didn't have time to fog over and threw on a pair of sweatpants and a sweatshirt. She glanced in the dining room mirror as she darted past. It wasn't pretty but at least she wasn't wearing her pajamas.

She slid her feet into her barn boots, grabbed her keys and jacket and raced out the door. The entire process had taken less than 15 minutes and by the time she got to Dot's, she knew Joe would be finishing his breakfast and working on his last cup of morning coffee before his shift started at 8:00.

Gloria slid Annabelle into an empty spot in front of Dot's and made a beeline for the front door. The place was packed and she could've sworn all eyes followed her across the room as she headed to Joe and his table for two in the corner.

She was certain Paul...and she...were the main topic of conversation. Gloria was a woman on a mission so she paid them no mind.

Gloria slid into the seat across from Joe, dropped her purse on the floor and leaned forward. "I need your help." There was no need to beat around the bush. Time was of the essence.

Officer Joe Nelson lifted his slice of whole-wheat toast and eyed her cautiously. He recognized the look in Gloria's eyes...the look of a desperate woman.

"What kind of help?" He chewed his toast, lifted his cup of coffee and studied her over the rim.

"I'm sure you know Paul is in trouble. I need someone who can get into Montbay County Sheriff's Station and – uh – look around."

Joe started to shake his head. "I'm not sure..."

"Look!" Gloria placed an open palm on the table. "Someone is trying to frame Paul. If I thought I could sneak in there myself, I wouldn't bother asking you, but I can't."

Officer Joe Nelson and Gloria locked eyes. He could hear the desperation in Gloria's voice and started to waffle.

"I dunno about this." He slowly shook his head. Joe liked Paul. He was a standup guy and Joe figured someone was trying to stick it to him. Still, Joe liked his job. Actually, Joe loved his job and the thought of putting his job in jeopardy for a friend, albeit a good one was not something he was ready to embrace.

Joe glanced around uneasily. It wouldn't be hard for someone at a table nearby to eavesdrop. The last thing he needed, if he decided to help Gloria, and he knew there was no way he could turn her down, not when she looked at him like that, was for someone to overhear their conversation.

He glanced at the check Holly, the server, had left on the table. He dropped a five and three ones on top of the check and slid his chair back. "Let's talk outside."

53

Gloria popped out of the chair and trailed behind as she followed him out the front door and onto the sidewalk. He stepped out of view of the large front picture window and motioned her off to the side. "Just once, Gloria. I'll help you this one time," he caved. "What do you want me to do?"

Gloria looked around, making sure they were alone. "Two things." She lifted an index finger. "One, I need you to get your hands on the notes. Not steal them. Just take a picture of them." She lifted a second finger. "Second, I need you to kind of put your ear to the ground, so to speak. See if you can figure out who is talking bad about Paul. You know, find out if anyone seems to be gloating..." she trailed off. She didn't want to come across as bossy, like she was trying to tell Joe what to do. After all, he was a cop. He should be able to sniff out the bad guys, even the ones he worked with.

Joe shoved his hands in his jacket pockets. "I'll see what I can do, Gloria, but don't get your hopes up," he warned.

Gloria nodded. "I won't," she promised. "I would appreciate any help, even a little."

He patted Gloria on the back. "I'll try, Gloria. The best I can do is try."

It was all Gloria could ask for, could hope for. She knew Joe would do what he could. She prayed it would be enough.

Joe glanced at his watch. "Gotta start my patrol now. I'll be at the station later this afternoon and when I get off duty later tonight, I'll stop by your place to let you know if I got the pictures and if I heard anything worth mentioning."

She watched as Joe climbed into his patrol car. He waved as he backed out of the parking spot and headed out of town. *Dear God. Please help Joe.*

Gloria started for the car. She abruptly changed direction and headed toward the post office. Maybe Ruth had heard something.

When she stepped into the lobby, she ran smack dab into Judith Arnett, who was on her way out.

Judith nodded at Gloria and sidestepped her as Gloria made her way to the counter. Judith and Gloria weren't the best of friends. Judith was a local gossip and, on more than one occasion, had nearly ruined a Belhaven resident's life with her malicious rumors.

Judith had mellowed out the last few years and it seemed to Gloria there were less rumors linked to Judith.

Gloria liked to believe that perhaps Judith had turned a new leaf and become a kinder, gentler, Judith.

Judith paused and then spun around. She took a tentative step toward Gloria. "I-I'm sorry about Paul," she said.

Gloria studied Judith's face. She seemed sincere. "I..."

A lump lodged in Gloria's throat and sudden tears burned the back of her eyes. She opened her mouth to reply to Judith's unexpected act of kindness and burst into tears. She lowered her head in her hands and sobbed.

Judith awkwardly placed an arm around Gloria's shoulders. "I-I'm sorry Gloria. I didn't mean to upset you..." She looked at Ruth helplessly.

Ruth bolted through the door that separated the lobby from the employee area and patted Gloria's back. "It's going to be okay, Gloria. We're here to help."

"Me, too," Judith chimed in. "I'll help if you want," she offered.

Ruth reached behind her and grabbed the box of Kleenex from the counter. She jerked several tissues from the box and put them in Gloria's hand.

Gloria dabbed her eyes and wiped her nose. "I'm sorry. I guess I'm stressed out."

Ruth slipped her arm through Gloria's and led her to the back.

Judith followed behind. "Ruth has been training me on her surveillance equipment," she said. "Just say the word."

Gloria's mind was mush. Other than asking Officer Joe Nelson to snoop around, she didn't have a plan, but she needed one.

"My cousin, Minnie, works part-time at Montbay Sheriff's Station in dispatch. Maybe she can help," Judith offered.

Gloria dabbed at her swollen eyes. It was a thought. The woman was probably a wealth of information. "Do you think I might be able to talk to her?"

Judith nodded. "Yep. I'll get right on it." She glanced at Ruth. "Maybe we could meet later tonight, have pizza and kind of butter her up."

"She loves food," Ruth explained.

"Y-you would do that for me?" Gloria wasn't sure if she was surprised or not.

Judith shifted her purse on her shoulder. "One time, right before Carl retired from the Montbay County Road Commission, someone tried to pin an accident on him. I know what it's like. It almost ruined our retirement." She looked at Ruth. "If not for Ruth butting in, he would have lost his pension, benefits, everything."

Gloria had never heard the story. It sounded a lot like what was happening to Paul, although Paul's circumstances were even direr since Paul could end up in jail!

"I'll bring the pizza," Gloria sniffled. "What time and where?"

"We can meet at my house," Judith said. "Carl is playing poker down at the VFW hall tonight so he'll be gone. Course I'll have to get ahold of Minnie first."

Judith promised to get right on it and call them to confirm. After Judith left the post office, Gloria hung back. "I don't know what to say, except thank God I ran into Judith."

Ruth crossed her arms and nodded. "Yep. She seems to have softened. Not sure why, though."

A customer walked inside the post office and approached the counter.

Gloria averted her eyes, reached inside her purse and grabbed her keys. "I'll talk to you later."

Gloria slipped out of the post office, crossed the street and climbed into her car. All she could do now was wait.

***

Gloria wandered aimlessly around the house. She needed busy work and decided the best thing she could do was bake. Baking always made her feel better. It kept her hands busy and on top of that, kept her out of trouble.

She waited anxiously for the phone to ring and when it finally did, she almost didn't answer, afraid of what bad news might be on the other end.

It was Judith. "We're on for 6:00 at my place," Judith told her when she picked up. "Bring a large, extra meat pizza for Minnie. I'm not picky so order whatever you want for Ruth, you and me."

Gloria grinned. "Minnie is going to eat an entire large pizza by herself?"

"Yep," Judith said. "Oh, and she loves those twisty breadsticks filled with gooey cheese."

"Let me guess. She can eat a whole box of those, too."

"Yep."

Gloria stepped over to the kitchen door and stared out into the yard. "What kind of pizza do you like, Judith?" She wanted to make sure Judith knew how much she appreciated her help.

"I'm not picky. The only things I don't like are olives," she admitted.

"Okay. I'll make sure there are no olives," Gloria assured her.

"See you at six."

Gloria started to say good-bye. "Judith!"

"Yeah?"

"Thanks. I mean. Really, thank you," Gloria could feel another meltdown coming on.

"You're welcome, Gloria." She hung up before Gloria could answer.

Gloria returned the handset to the cradle and reached for her apron. It was time to make her grandsons' all-time favorite holiday treat – Christmas cookies.

Gloria pulled a set of mixing bowls from the cupboard. Next, she assembled the sugars, the flour, the butter and the eggs. She spread everything on the counters and began measuring out the ingredients. After mixing the ingredients, she switched on the radio and turned it to a Christmas classics station.

Gloria smiled as she pulled out the tin with the cookie cutters. The cookie cutters were the same ones her children and she had used to make the special cookies when they were young.

She sprinkled flour on the counter, rolled out the dough and cut the cookies into various shapes. There were reindeer, Christmas trees, snowmen, gingerbread men, stars and angels. She picked up a spatula and carefully transferred the cookies from the counter to the cookie sheets. After loading three sheets full, she placed the cookies inside the preheated oven and shut the oven door.

While the cookies baked, Gloria mixed the ingredients for the frosting. James, Gloria's husband, had loved the Christmas cookies and his favorite part was the frosting, until he found out the main ingredient was shortening. She tried to explain the shortening was what made it creamy, but after that, he didn't care for them as much.

Her children and grandchildren did. She couldn't remember if Paul liked Christmas cookies and in fact, couldn't remember if she had even made them for him.

When the cookies finished baking, Gloria pulled them from the oven and placed the sheets on top of the stove. After they cooled, she separated the frosting into four separate bowls and squeezed drops of food coloring in three of them. There was a bowl of green, a bowl of red, a bowl of blue and then she left one bowl white.

She spread thick layers of creamy frosting on each of the cookies and then decorated the tops with sprinkles, colorful dots and cinnamon candies. Her daughter, Jill, didn't care for the toppings so she left a few plain.

It took another hour to clean up the mess. After the kitchen was spic and span, she headed to the bathroom to wash up.

Gloria placed her pizza order with Joe, who owned Guiseppe's Pizza. "Can you please deliver the pizzas to Judith Arnett's place?"

Joe paused. "Did you say Judith Arnett?" Everyone in the small Town of Belhaven knew Gloria and Judith weren't the best of friends, including Joe Guiseppe.

"Yep. We're having pizza at her place." She didn't go into detail but knew Joe was most certainly wondering why on earth Gloria was eating pizza at Judith's place.

She gave him her credit card information, told him to add a $10 tip and then headed for the door.

Gloria couldn't wait to find out what Minnie Dexter had to say!

Chapter 6

Ruth's van was already in Judith's drive when Gloria pulled up out front. Parked in the drive was another vehicle Gloria didn't recognize. She guessed the vehicle belonged to Minnie.

Both the front porch and the side porch lights were on. Gloria climbed out of the car and squeezed past the cars as she made her way to the side porch.

Ruth, who had been waiting for Gloria to arrive, flung the door open and stepped to the side to let her in.

Gloria had been in Judith's place once before, when Judith helped solve a case that involved Ruth.

Beyond the small mudroom was a large, open kitchen. Sitting at the kitchen table was Judith and a woman with jet-black hair and olive-colored skin. The woman turned, her dark brown eyes honing in on Gloria.

Judith smiled. "Hello Gloria. You're right on time."

Gloria returned the smile. "I ordered the pizzas from Guiseppe's. I hope that's okay."

Judith nodded. "I love Guiseppe's." She pointed to the woman seated next to her. "Minnie, this is Gloria. Gloria, this is my cousin, Minnie."

Minnie half-smiled. "Ah, so you are the infamous Gloria Rutherford, super sleuth."

Gloria shrugged out of her coat and hung it on the back of an empty chair. Whatever she had expected Minnie to look like...this wasn't it. She was thin, even thinner than Lucy was if she had to guess. She was also tall, with long arms and gangly legs that stuck out from under the table.

"Yes and it seems I need your help." There was no sense in mincing words. She might as well get down to business.

Minnie patted her tummy. "I don't work well on an empty stomach."

Judith agreed. "Minnie will want to eat first and then we can discuss the case."

Gloria frowned. There was no "case." Someone has set Paul up. Gloria intended to find out who had it in for him. Simple.

Still, she needed Minnie...happy and willing to talk. "Yes, of course."

Judith, Ruth and Gloria made small talk while Minnie remained silent. She wasn't kidding when she said she wanted to eat.

Thankfully, the Guiseppe's delivery driver arrived a short time later.

Ruth met him at the door and handed the pizzas off to Gloria, who carried them to the table while Judith placed a small stack of paper plates and napkins in the center.

Minnie reached for a box. "Which one is mine?" She didn't wait for an answer but lifted the lid on the first one and scrunched her nose. "Yuck. Mushrooms. That one is definitely not mine."

She shoved the box across the table and reached for the next one.

Gloria held her breath as Minnie peeked inside.

Minnie nodded. The pizza passed inspection. "Yep. This is it." She didn't bother with a plate but instead, yanked a piece of pizza from the box, lifted it to her mouth and took a big bite. She wolfed down the first slice, then the second slice before taking a breather. "I thought there were breadsticks, too. This little pizza isn't going to fill me up."

Gloria's eyes widened. Where in the world did this woman put her food? The other three watched in silence as the one-woman eating machine devoured her entire large pizza, a box of cheesy breadsticks and then reached for another other pie.

Gloria had ordered a third pizza as a spare – cheese only – and it was a good thing she had! The eating machine was still hungry.

Minnie frowned at the cheese-only pizza. "Who orders a pizza with only cheese?"

"Me," Gloria said in a small voice. "I didn't know you would want extra."

Judith gave her a dark look.

Gloria clamped her mouth shut. She hoped she hadn't offended Minnie.

Minnie paid no mind as she ate two slices of cheese pizza and one more breadstick. She glanced at Judith. "What's for dessert?"

Gloria looked down at her own plate. She had just started on her second slice of pizza and taken a single bite of her breadstick.

Minnie had polished off an entire large meat lover's pizza, two slices of cheese pizza, a box of breadsticks and she was still hungry.

Judith shook her head. "I-I have some leftover cinnamon rolls from breakfast," she offered.

Minnie frowned. "Well, if that's all you've got."

Judith scrambled out of the chair, darted over to the fridge and slid the tin of cinnamon rolls off the top. She handed them to Minnie, who removed the plastic wrapper, peeled a cinnamon roll from the pack and shoved it in her mouth. The whole thing. At once.

Gloria guessed she had to be close to full because she slowed considerably while eating the second cinnamon roll. When she got to the third roll, she nibbled the edge. "I don't think I can swallow another bite, but I'll take it home if you don't mind."

She eyed the leftover pizza on the table. "That, too, if you're not gonna eat it. I'll need a snack before I go to bed."

Gloria's stomach churned. If she had eaten as much food as Minnie had in one sitting, she would be in a food coma!

Minnie reached for a napkin and dabbed at the corners of her mouth. "Now. You were wondering if I've heard any scuttlebutt at the station about Paul's...untimely investigation."

Gloria nodded eagerly. "Yes. Whatever tidbit of information you might have, no matter how small you think it might be, could be helpful." She reached inside her purse, pulled out her trusty notepad and pen and flipped the pad open.

Minnie nodded and sipped her soda. "Rumor has been circulating for a good month now that something big was about to go down at the station. At first, I heard it had something to do with one of the rookies."

Minnie twisted the napkin in her hand thoughtfully. "Was it Jason or Alex?" She stared at the ceiling, as if a face, either Jason or Alex's, would materialize. She lowered her gaze and looked at Gloria. "It had to be Jason. Yeah, it was Jason."

She shrugged. "Anyway, Pearl. Pearl Johnson, the other dispatcher, and I were making bets...friendly, mind you, on who was about to get taken down."

Minnie lifted the glass of soda to her lips, tipped her head back and downed the contents. She lowered her head and then rattled the ice cubes inside the glass. "Got anymore? I'm parched."

Once again, Judith jumped out of her seat and darted to the fridge. Gloria made a mental note to do something nice...extra nice...for Judith!

Minnie waited for Judith to fill her empty glass and then took a big gulp before she continued. "Well, imagine our surprise when Paul Kennedy was put on leave after Captain Davies searched his locker and found the cash and notes."

She shook her head in disbelief. "Never in a million years would I have suspected Officer Kennedy...Paul."

"Alex and Paul patrolled together," Gloria prompted.

Minnie nodded. "Yep. Not often. Paul either patrolled with Alex Tisdale or Stan Woszinski."

Gloria remembered Stan was the balding officer, closer to Paul's age and retirement.

Minnie lifted the leftover cinnamon roll and nibbled the side. "Guess I had a little room left in the ole tummy, after all."

Watching Minnie eat more food caused Gloria to feel nauseous.

Minnie popped the last of the cinnamon roll in her mouth and washed it down with a couple swigs of soda. She wiped her hands on the front of her slacks.

"I would have guessed Alex had somehow managed to set Paul up but he didn't."

"Why not?" Ruth asked.

Minnie shrugged. "Cuz Alex was fired two days before the cash and bribery notes were found in Paul's locker."

***

Judith, anticipating Minnie's demand for more soda, poured her glass full.

Minnie shook her head. "Whew! I'm getting full."

Finally.

She eyed the glass of soda. "Waste not, want not." She chugged the glass and set it back on the table. "Yeah. Alex was kind of a troublemaker. I could see his days were numbered."

"How did he get fired?" Judith asked.

Minnie opened her mouth and then clamped it shut. "I don't know how much I should say."

Ruth leaned in. "We'll keep it amongst ourselves." She made a zipping motion across her lips.

"Well..." She eyed Judith uneasily. "I caught him at a strip club and told Captain Davies." She hurried on. "The place is well known all over Green Springs. I pass by there each night I work and I happened to see Alex's pick-up truck parked off to the side."

Minnie wiggled in her chair. "So I parked my car behind the oil change place. It's right next door to the strip club," she explained. "Guess my instinct for investigation comes from working in police dispatch. It's in my blood."

"You caught him coming out," Gloria prompted.

Minnie nodded. "Yep. Sure as sugar. He was drunker than a skunk, too, swaying and staggering. He climbed into his truck and I thought for sure he was gonna get into an accident so I followed him home."

This woman was a girl after Gloria's own heart. Not the food part, the investigating part.

Minnie tsk-tsked. "He got home alright but only by the grace of God."

Minnie swirled the melting ice cubes around in her glass. "Anyhoo, I told Captain Davies and next thing I know Alex is gone." She thumbed her finger out. "Lickety-split."

Ruth drummed her fingers on top of the table. "It could be Alex believed Paul had turned him in and decided to get even with him by setting him up."

Gloria picked up. "So he blackmailed Cal Evergreen, City Commissioner, along with Mitzi Verona and made it look like Paul did it."

Minnie nodded. "The case is bigger than Commissioner Evergreen and Ms. Verona. There were several other people blackmailed."

She sucked in a breath. "Not that you heard me say anything."

Gloria shook her head and made a zipping motion. "Mums the word."

This meant the investigation - and Paul's suspension - could go on indefinitely. Gloria's dream of a beautiful winter wedding was slipping away.

Ruth noticed the look on Gloria's face. She reached out and patted her hand. "Don't worry, Gloria. We're gonna kick this investigation into high gear."

Minnie pushed back her chair, grabbed the leftover pizza and reached for her purse. "I best get going. I have to let Jupiter out and make my lunch for tomorrow."

Gloria could only imagine what Minnie ate for lunch. She probably needed a U-Haul® truck to get it to the station!

The trio watched Minnie as she walked to her car.

Judith turned to Gloria. "What do you think?"

"I smell a skunk. Maybe it was Alex. Maybe it wasn't."

"It sure sounds like Alex," Ruth said.

"True," Gloria admitted. "Minnie seemed determined to pin it on him."

Minnie backed her car out of the drive and onto the road.

Gloria crossed her arms in front of her. "There's something Miss Minnie isn't telling us. I can feel it."

Chapter 7

Gloria left shortly after Minnie. She wandered into the kitchen and walked over to the home phone, anxious to see if perhaps Paul had called. It had been two days since he had hinted that they might need to postpone the wedding.

Lucy and Margaret told her earlier they had stopped by his place to try to talk to him. They found his truck parked in the drive but no one answered when they knocked on the door.

The light on the machine was blinking red. She pushed the button and listened to the first message.

"Hi Mom. I wanted to remind you about tomorrow night and the boys' Christmas program at church. You can meet us there around quarter to seven. It starts at seven."

Gloria tilted her head back and closed her eyes. She had completely forgotten Tyler and Ryan were in their church's Christmas play, "One Starry Night."

She slid open the silverware drawer and lifted the tray. She had tucked the invitation in a safe place and then completely forgotten about it.

Gloria pulled the colorful Christmas invitation out, slipped her reading glasses on and studied the front. Sure enough, the program started at seven the following evening at Pilgrim Bible Church in Green Springs!

She quickly called Jill back. "Yes, dear. I forgot all about the program," Gloria told her daughter.

"I hope you can make it," Jill replied. "The boys are practicing their little hearts out and they asked me to call you to make sure you would be there."

Gloria wouldn't miss it for the world! She didn't care what kind of personal crisis she was smack dab in the middle of. There was no way she would let Ryan and Tyler down.

"I'll be there," she answered firmly. She promised to meet Jill and Greg in front of the church entrance at 6:45 the following evening and then hung up the phone.

There was one more voice message on Gloria's phone. It was Margaret.

"Hi Gloria. I stopped by earlier but you weren't home. Lucy and I ran by Paul's place again this evening and his truck was gone. It looks..."

Margaret paused. "Look, give me a call. I want to stop by and talk to you."

Gloria had a gut feeling whatever Margaret had to say was not good.

She immediately picked up the phone and called Margaret's cell phone.

Margaret picked up on the first ring. "You at home?"

"Yeah. What is going on?" Gloria asked.

"I'd rather not talk on the phone," Margaret replied. "Can I come over?"

Gloria paused for a brief moment. On the one hand, she wasn't in the mood for company. On the other hand, there was no way she would be able to sleep, wondering what Margaret deemed important enough to drop everything she was doing to come over.

The latter won out. "Sure. I'll be here."

"I'm on my way." The line went dead and Gloria stared at the phone in her hand. Her heart began to pound and her pulse raced as she paced the kitchen floor.

It was as if she were in the middle of a bad dream. She pinched her arm and winced at the pain. Nope. She was wide-awake, unfortunately.

Mally scrambled out of her doggie bed and trotted to the door. Mally was the unofficial doorbell.

Gloria flipped on the porch light and peeked out the window. Margaret had brought reinforcement. Lucy was with her. The feeling of dread turned to impending doom. It was going to be worse than Gloria thought, of that she was certain.

She unlocked the door and slowly pulled it open.

Gloria held the door as Margaret and Lucy wiped their shoes on the rug before stepping into the kitchen. "Should I make coffee?"

Margaret nodded. "Got any Captain Morgan to throw in it?"

Lucy whacked Margaret's arm. "Margaret!"

Margaret shrugged. "She might need it."

Gloria turned her attention to the coffee pot. "You're scaring me. What is going on?"

Lucy unwound the scarf from her neck and laid it in the chair. She slipped out of her coat and slid into a kitchen chair before casting Margaret an uneasy glance.

Gloria measured out the coffee, put it into a filter, poured fresh water into the reservoir and flipped the switch to "on" before settling in at the table and fixing her gaze on her two friends. "This has to do with Paul. What happened?"

Lucy tugged on the collar of her shirt. "We, uh, stopped by Paul's place earlier."

"Did you talk to him? I haven't heard from him since the day he left here."

"No," Margaret admitted. "We didn't."

"His truck wasn't there?" Gloria probed. Getting these two to talk was like pulling teeth.

"Uh-uh. Paul's son, Jeff, was there." Margaret popped out of the chair and headed over to the coffee pot.

"Did you talk to him?" It was twenty questions...going nowhere. "What did he say?"

Margaret poured three cups of coffee, carried two to the table, set one in front of Lucy and the other in front of Gloria before returning for the third.

Margaret grabbed her cup and eased into the chair next to Gloria. "I don't know how to say this."

"Spit it out," Gloria said.

"Paul left town," Lucy blurted out.

***

Gloria's eyes widened and her mouth fell open. "Left town?" She blinked rapidly as she tried to digest the news.

Margaret nodded uneasily. "Jeff told us Paul packed a large suitcase, tossed it into his pick-up truck and drove off. He wouldn't say where he went."

"W-when did he leave?" Gloria had officially been jilted! Her world tumbled around her. Was he guilty, after all? Why else would he turn tail and run?

Here Gloria was, trying to clear his name and he wasn't even around! Never in a million years would she have guessed him to be not only a criminal, but also a quitter!

Gloria shook her head, as if to clear it. "Well, I guess it's settled, then. If he's not interested in clearing his name, why should I?"

Lucy waved her hand across the tabletop. "We don't know he isn't interested. We don't even know where he went," she argued.

"You would think he would've at least told his children where he was going," Gloria pointed out.

Margaret shrugged her shoulders. "Maybe he did and told them not to tell."

Gloria's brows formed a "v." It was possible he had stumbled onto something. Still, wouldn't he have at least had the common courtesy to call Gloria to let her know he was leaving town? After all, they were engaged to be married! Or had been, she reminded herself.

The girls weren't able to offer any more information. They stayed until they were sure Gloria would be all right and promised to check in with her first thing in the morning.

Snow began to fall and when Gloria opened the back door, a gust of arctic air and snow blew in. The girls hustled to Lucy's jeep and quickly jumped in.

Gloria waved as they pulled out of the drive and then slowly closed the door behind them.

She leaned her forehead against the coolness of the glass and closed her eyes as tears streamed down her cheeks. What should have been the happiest time in her life was turning out to be one of the worst. In fact, she wasn't sure how it could possibly get worse.

If only she knew...

Chapter 8

Gloria climbed into bed and pulled the covers over her head. Puddles wasn't having any of that as he wiggled his way under the blankets and cuddled up next to Gloria. His purr soothed her frazzled nerves and despite her broken heart, she promptly fell into a deep slumber.

The next morning, she woke with a renewed determination to clear Paul's name! Maybe he was onto something and didn't want to drag anyone else into it, just like he didn't want to marry Gloria with a black cloud hanging over his head.

She rolled out of bed, grabbed a pair of jeans, along with a festive red holiday sweater to match the mood she was determined to have and headed to the bathroom.

In the shower, she plotted her day. She reminded herself she needed to be at Pilgrim Bible Church that evening to watch Ryan and Tyler.

The first thing she planned to do was drive to Paul's house and demand that Jeff tell her where his father had gone. She had a right to know!

Next, she was going to track down Officer Joe Nelson to see if he'd been able to get a picture of the blackmail letters Paul had supposedly written. Maybe he'd been able to glean other information, as well.

Afterward, she would come home and start her online searches.

Gloria finished showering and quickly dressed before heading to the kitchen. She sipped her morning coffee and pulled out her handy dandy pad of paper. First, there was Alex. She slid her reading glasses on and leaned in. Alex Tisdale. The young cop who had been fired.

The next on the list was Paul's other patrol partner, Stan something "ski." The name was spelled Woszinski, but Gloria wasn't sure on correct pronunciation.

Her eyes wandered down the list. Jason Endres. Gloria tapped her finger on top of the pad. Minnie had mentioned Jason was not a fan of Paul's. She wondered what Paul had ever done to cause the young officer to dislike him. Maybe he had gotten in trouble...

Next was Diane Stone, the woman who had been after Paul. Gloria's eyes narrowed. Four cops. Four possible motives. Three of the four had opportunity and access to the locker room.

Gloria finished her coffee, forced herself to eat a bowl of cold cereal and headed for the door.

She slipped into her winter coat, zipped the front, reached for her purse and opened the back door where she came face-to-face with Dot, who stood on the other side, her hand raised in a fist, ready to knock.

"Where are you going?" Dot blinked rapidly. It was only eight o'clock in the morning.

"Why are you here?" Gloria asked.

"To...uh..." Dot fumbled with her words.

"Lucy and Margaret told you to come over here and keep an eye on me," Gloria correctly guessed.

"Well, they were, uh..."

Gloria stomped her foot. "I'm a grown adult and perfectly capable of..."

"Getting yourself in a whole heap of trouble." Dot finished her sentence.

"So they sent the ever sensible, level-headed, no-nonsense Dot Jenkins to keep tabs on me."

Dot shifted her gaze. "Something like that." She slipped her hands in her coat pockets. "We're concerned, Gloria."

Gloria shouldn't be mad...in fact she couldn't be mad. Her friends were only watching out for her. She should be grateful, not grumbling.

Gloria turned her frown upside down, determined to start her day on the right foot. She patted Dot's arm. "Well, we aren't going to sit around waiting for spring to arrive."

She sidestepped Dot and pulled the door shut behind her. "We have stuff to do."

Dot took a deep breath and braced herself for what was to come. "I can hardly wait," she groaned.

Dot waited for Gloria to back Annabelle out of the garage before she slid into the passenger seat and reached for the seatbelt. There was a thick layer of snow on the grass but the air had started to warm and although the roads were wet, they weren't covered in snow or ice.

"Where we headed?" Dot asked.

Gloria looked both ways and pulled the car out onto the road. "First, we're going to Paul's place to find out where he went."

Dot gazed at her friend. Lucy and Margaret had filled her in on their visit to Paul's and how his son couldn't - or wouldn't - tell them where his father had gone. "You think he'll tell you?"

Gloria gripped the steering wheel with both hands, her mouth set in a grim line. "I give it a 50/50 chance he'll spill the beans. If he even knows," she added.

"True." Dot stared out the window. She wasn't nearly as hands-on in Gloria's investigations as the others were. She had a sneaky suspicion the other Garden Girls had sent her because Dot had a softer approach versus some of the others who were a little more outspoken.

The drive to Paul's farm didn't take long. Gloria pulled into the drive and noticed an older minivan she didn't recognize.

Paul's truck was nowhere in sight.

Gloria pulled off to the side and slid out of the driver's seat. "I'll be right back."

Dot watched through the front windshield as Gloria walked around the front of the car and up the side steps to the porch door.

Gloria rang the bell and waited. Moments later, the door inched open. Jeff, Paul's son, took one look at Gloria and swung the door open. "Gloria."

Gloria shifted her feet. "Hi Jeff. I, uh, know your father is gone and was, uh, wondering if you could tell me where he went."

She could tell from the expression on his face he was torn.

Gloria pressed on. "He may be in some kind of trouble or walking into a dangerous situation."

Jeff twisted the doorknob in his hand as he weighed his options. He would never forgive himself if Gloria was right and his father was in trouble. "He went to Lansing."

Gloria frowned. Lansing, Michigan was Michigan's capital city. What in the world would he be doing there? "Did he say how long he'd be gone?"

Jeff shook his head. "Nope." He leaned against the doorjamb. "In fact, he didn't tell me where he was going. He was in kind of a hurry to leave and left a computer screen open. He had made a hotel reservation."

"Do you remember the name of the hotel?"

Jeff nodded. "Yep, in fact, I wrote it down, just in case. Hang on." Jeff disappeared inside the house and returned a few moments later. He handed Gloria a slip of paper.

Gloria glanced at the paper and shoved it in her jacket pocket.

"Thank you, Jeff." Gloria impulsively reached up and kissed her soon-to-be (at least she hoped) stepson's cheek.

Jeff blushed. "You're welcome Gloria."

Gloria turned to go.

"My dad. He's stubborn as a mule sometimes," he called out.

Gloria turned, a half-smile on her face. "That's okay," she said. "So am I."

Back inside the car, Gloria turned the GPS on and punched in the address. "Paul is in Lansing," she told Dot.

The GPS calculated the location and informed them it would take over an hour to get there.

Dot squinted at the screen. "This is a hotel. Maybe we should call to make sure he's there," she pointed out.

Gloria nodded. "Good idea." She turned the car onto the road and headed back home.

Gloria pulled Annabelle into the drive, parked off to the side and wandered up the steps with Dot.

"What is that?" Dot reached out and plucked a folded piece of paper tucked in the doorframe. She unfolded the piece of paper and stared at the words.

Gloria shoved the key in the lock and twisted the knob. "What does it say?"

"It's a note from Officer Joe Nelson. He said he sent you a text. He wants to talk to you ASAP. He left a number."

Gloria turned the knob and pushed the kitchen door open. She promptly dropped her purse on the chair, reached inside and pulled out her cell phone. Sure enough, there was a new text message.

She pressed the message button and tapped the screen.

Gloria looked up at Dot. "He got it! He sent me pictures of the extortion notes Paul had supposedly written!"

There was also a missed call...from Paul. Her heart sank when she realized he hadn't left a message.

Gloria quickly dialed his cell phone and it went right to voice mail. She had no idea what to say so she didn't leave a message, either. Her lower lip quivered. "I missed Paul's call." At least he had tried to call.

With a determined effort, Gloria focused on Joe's message. She switched back to the text message and quickly forwarded the pictures to her email address, kicked her snow boots off, threw her jacket on the chair and darted into the dining room.

Dot was hot on her heels. Maybe they were making progress!

Gloria fired up the computer and tapped the desk impatiently as she waited for it to warm up. "I think it's time for a new computer. This thing is ancient and slower than molasses."

The only reason Gloria hadn't purchased a new one yet was because she wasn't tech savvy. She was waiting for her oldest son, Eddie, to arrive. He was up on all of the newest gadgets and gizmos and had promised to hook her up.

Finally, the machine came to life and Gloria went right to her email. She opened the one from Officer Joe Nelson and enlarged the screen.

There were two notes; both of them typed:

"Put twenty-five thousand dollars in unmarked bills in the trashcan next to the gazebo in Besterman Park by midnight tonight or else I go public with the pictures of you and Pandora Gillette at noon tomorrow." The note was initialed PK.

Gloria jabbed her finger on the screen. "This does not make Paul the culprit," she fumed. "Someone set him up."

Dot slid her reading glasses on and peered over Gloria's shoulder at the screen. "What does the second note say?"

The second note was addressed to Mitzi Verona, the wealthy widow of developer Percival Verona. The note demanded fifty thousand dollars in unmarked bills, twice as much as the one addressed to Commissioner Evergreen and the location was different. Whoever was extorting the money was smart enough to change locations.

Gloria was surprised at the drop location for the cash. It was outside the Green Springs Library, although the extortionist instructed Mitzi to put the cash in a paper sack and place it behind the bushes in the back of the library.

Someone obviously knew there were no surveillance cameras. After all, who would break into a library to steal a bunch of books?

The signature was the same, *PK*.

If Paul had received $75k in cash, he sure hadn't acted like it! Gloria didn't believe for a second Paul was involved.

Gloria clicked out of the screen and reached for her cell phone. She called the number Officer Joe Nelson had given her. He didn't answer so she left him a message. After she left the message, she sent him a text.

"Now what?" Dot asked.

"We wait for Officer Joe Nelson."

Gloria headed to the fridge. She opened the door and peered inside. It was slim pickins'. There was a half a package of sliced cheddar cheese and an unopened container of cottage cheese and some leftovers.

Inside the cupboard, Gloria grabbed a can of tomato basil soup and a loaf of bread. "I hope you don't mind grilled cheese sandwiches and canned soup," Gloria said.

Dot waved a hand. "As long as I'm not cookin', I could care less."

Gloria wandered over to the counter, popped the top on the can of soup, dumped the contents into a saucepan and set it on the burner before turning the burner on.

She sprayed butter spray on four slices of bread. Gloria changed her mind and made it six slices when she saw two sets of hungry eyes gazing up at her.

When the food was ready, Gloria tore one of the grilled cheese sandwiches apart and broke some of it into bite-size pieces for Puddles and put the rest of the sandwich in Mally's dish.

She hadn't even settled into her chair before her beloved pets had wolfed down their treats and begged for more.

"Oh no!" Gloria pointed to the other room. "We want to eat in peace." Her furry housemates slunk out of the kitchen and Dot grinned. "Every time Odie looks at Ray like that, Ray pulls out the chair and invites him to the table."

Gloria chuckled. Odie had come from the puppy mill Gloria and her friends had discovered a couple months earlier. Odie and Ray, Dot's husband, bonded immediately. She had to admit that Odie was quite a character and had a way of looking at you that melted your heart.

Mally and Puddles did the same thing. If Gloria wasn't careful, they would be running the show, as if they weren't already.

Dot reached for Gloria's hand. "Let's pray."

Gloria nodded and lowered her head. "Dear Lord. We pray You will help us clear Paul's name. We know he is innocent and ask You to lead us to the real culprit and fast, if You don't mind, so Gloria and Paul can marry."

Tears stung the back of Gloria's eyes as she lifted her head. "Thanks Dot. Your prayer means a lot."

Dot reached over and patted Gloria's hand. "I feel at peace about this. God has it all under control."

As the girls munched on their lunch, Gloria asked Dot how her cancer treatments were going. Dot was in the midst of radiation treatment and her prognosis was good. Gloria had prayed for her dear friend every day and God was answering all of her prayers.

"Good." Dot tore off a piece of her sandwich and dipped it in her bowl of soup. "It makes me tired," she admitted.

Gloria had no idea what Dot had gone – or was going - through. She could see Dot tired easily. "Maybe you should go home and rest instead of babysitting me."

Dot reached for her soupspoon. "You aren't going to get rid of me that easy," she teased.

After they finished their lunch, the girls rinsed the dirty dishes and placed them inside the dishwasher.

Gloria had no more than closed the dishwasher door when she heard a light tap on the porch door. She peeked out the window. It was Officer Joe Nelson.

Gloria swung the door open and stepped to the side.

Officer Joe Nelson snatched the hat off his head. "Boy, you're not gonna believe what I found out!"

Chapter 9

Gloria grabbed his hand and pulled him into the kitchen. "I hope it's good news!" she exclaimed. She was due for a break in the case. It was wearing her down. It seemed as if she was running in circles and going nowhere.

Gloria pulled out a kitchen chair. "Here, have a seat. Coffee?"

She knew she was rambling but she had a feeling Officer Joe Nelson had news...big news, judging by the look on his face.

He glanced at Dot, seated on the other side of the table. "Hi Dot."

"Hello Joe." Dot and Officer Joe Nelson were on a first name basis. After all, he was in the restaurant every morning like clockwork.

"I'll take a cup of coffee, if you don't mind."

"Not at all." Gloria rushed over to the coffee pot, dumped some fresh grounds in the filter and filled the pot with water. She poured the water in the reservoir and then turned it on.

She darted over to the table, slid out the chair and plopped down. "What 'cha got?"

"Whew!" Joe scratched his forehead. "I think I blew open a hornet's nest."

He went on. "Poor Paul. Man, he has a bunch of people gunning for his arrest."

"Like who?" Gloria asked.

"Well, there's the young rookie, Jason Endres. Alex Tisdale, the other rookie who just got fired filed a complaint." Gloria wasn't surprised by either name. "Anyone else?"

Joe shook his head. "Believe it or not, even Captain Davies seems convinced Paul was involved."

Gloria's heart sank. Captain Davies. Paul's boss!

"I couldn't get close to Paul's locker, though. Seems every time I went in there, someone was lurking around." He snorted. "It was almost as if it was being guarded."

If there were evidence inside Paul's locker, it would be long gone so maybe it didn't matter as much as Gloria had originally thought. Still, someone in the sheriff's station knew something at the very least...or more importantly, was the real extortionist.

Gloria clenched her fist and pounded the table in frustration. "If there was only some way to snoop around inside the police station without raising suspicion."

Joe leaned back in the chair and crossed his arms. "Well, I've been thinkin' and I have an idea."

"What?"

"Montbay hired this new cleaning service a couple months back. They come in at night and empty trash, sweep the floors, stuff like that."

Dot perked up. "Let me guess. You know someone who works for the cleaning company."

Joe ginned. "Yep. It's my cousin, Kim. She's one of the supervisors." He pulled a slip of paper from his front shirt pocket and handed it to Gloria. "I told her I needed to get a friend or two in there to work temporarily."

He pointed to the slip of paper. "That's her name and number. Give Kim a call and she'll hook you up."

Gloria popped out of her chair, reached over and hugged Joe. "Thank you, thank you, thank you! I take back all those things I said about you." She winked.

Joe slid his chair back and stood. "Now don't go getting into trouble."

Dot snorted. "Gloria? Trouble?"

Gloria gave her a dark look.

Joe held up a hand. "You're safe with Kim. She won't breathe a word, not even to her crew."

"I'll be epitome of discreet," Gloria promised. "Can I take someone with me?"

Joe's eyes slid to Dot. "Yeah. Maybe one other person. Not Lucy, though. She's a firecracker. I can see her pulling out a pistol and shooting someone."

"I'll do it," Dot offered.

Joe shook his head. "Only problem is a lot of the other officers know you."

That was true. Gloria frowned.

"Margaret might work," Dot suggested.

Lucy was out.

Ruth was out. Not only did she work at the post office, she would also be easily recognized.

Dot was out.

That left either Andrea or Margaret. Andrea might work. Gloria quickly dismissed her young friend. She was cute as a button but she would draw too much attention, especially from the young rookies. It would have to be Margaret.

Gloria hugged Joe one more time and then watched as he headed back to his patrol car and climbed into the driver's seat. Gloria's heart lurched as she watched him. It reminded her of Paul and his patrol car. She slowly closed the door and turned to Dot. "I guess we better get Margaret on the horn."

Gloria phoned Kim and arranged for the short-term cleaning assignment. She was relieved that Kim didn't ask any questions and even told Gloria to give her a call if something came up and she couldn't make it.

Next on her list was a call to Margaret. It took some wheedling but Gloria was finally able to convince Margaret to accompany her on her fact-finding mission. After she hung up the phone, she glanced at the clock.

"Ryan and Tyler are in the Christmas play at their church this evening and I can't miss it," she told Dot.

Dot slid out of the seat and reached for her purse. "I best get back to the restaurant and check on Ray and Holly anyway." She hugged Gloria tightly and then headed for the door.

After Dot left, Gloria took a long, leisurely bath as she thought about Paul and wondered what was going on. She believed in her heart he was trying to protect her. Still, she missed him desperately and it felt as if someone had tilted her world and he was the only one who could right it.

Gloria quickly warmed some leftovers and pulled the morning paper she hadn't even touched, across the table to read the headlines while she ate. She glanced at the front page and pushed the paper away. It was full of gloom and doom. The only thing the news reported on anymore was the bad stuff. They never reported on the good in people.

She finished eating, rinsed her dirty plate and placed it inside the dishwasher.

Gloria left the light above the stove on, flipped the porchlight on and headed to the car. It was dark and she avoided driving at night if possible, but tonight, she made an exception. She wouldn't miss Ryan and Tyler's performance for the world.

Jill was waiting near the front entrance of the church. "Greg is saving us a couple seats." She tucked her arm through her mother's arm and turned to head in. "Paul couldn't make it?"

Gloria frowned. "No. He, uh. He couldn't." Gloria left it at that. She didn't want to lie nor did she want to go into a long, drawn out explanation.

On the drive over, she had determined to set the whole thing aside and focus on the reason for the season, Jesus' birth. She also wanted to take a mental break and enjoy watching her grandsons.

Jill shuffled into the pew and settled in next to Greg. Gloria squeezed in and sat on the other side of Jill. The seats were perfect. Gloria had an unobstructed view of the manger, the stable and the twinkling stars strategically placed above the Nativity scene.

Gloria hadn't asked, and Jill hadn't told her mother, what part the boys had in the play. She wanted it to be a surprise.

The music started and the audience quieted. To the left, from behind the curtain, emerged a miniature Joseph and Mary. Mary cradled a child wrapped in a blanket.

The music picked up the tempo and "Away in the Manger" played. Mary rocked the "baby" which Gloria quickly realized was a doll while "Joseph" looked on.

A movement to the right caught Gloria's attention. The curtain swayed and out walked the three wise men, wearing crowns on their heads, dressed in long, purple robes, tied at the waist with twined belts of gold. Three beards of white covered their small faces.

Gloria narrowed her eyes and studied them. She recognized two of the wise men...Tyler and Ryan.

Tyler spoke first. "Is this the child we have been searching for?" The wise men shuffled across the stage and approached the Nativity scene.

Bright stage lights beamed down on the Nativity. Ryan, the middle wise man, shaded his eyes. "It is…" He paused, blinking rapidly. "The lights…they're blinding me," he said.

The crowd tittered. The third wise man tried to cover. "That must be the Star of Bethlehem."

"Nope," Ryan argued. "It's the stage lights!"

Tyler tried to help his younger brother by nudging Ryan out of the spotlight. Instead, he stepped on the hem of his own long robe and started to lose his balance.

Tyler's arms flailed wildly in the air as he tried to regain his balance. He grabbed the first thing his fingers made contact…with Ryan's "beard." He yanked his brother's beard off and tumbled backward onto the stage floor.

"My beard!" Ryan lunged forward in a desperate attempt to retrieve his beard and landed in a heap on top of his brother.

The crowd burst out laughing.

The lights quickly lowered, the boys scrambled to their feet, adjusted their clothing and the play continued, as if nothing had ever happened.

After it ended, Jill, Greg and Gloria headed backstage.

Tyler was nowhere in sight.

Ryan was sitting nearby on the floor. He had removed his crown and was spinning it like a top on the stage floor.

Gloria crouched down and patted his head. "You were one of the handsomest wise men I have ever seen," she said.

Ryan shoved his chin on his fist and frowned. "Tyler ruined it," he pouted.

Gloria shook her head. "He was trying to help you." She quickly changed the subject. "Did you make out your list for Santa Claus yet?"

Tyler had been telling Ryan there was no Santa Claus but Gloria knew he still believed, at least a little.

Ryan brightened. His head bobbed up and down. "Yep! I asked for a BB Gun."

Gloria lifted her gaze and looked at her daughter questioningly. Jill gave a slight shake of her head and Gloria let out a sigh of relief. She hoped he wouldn't be too disappointed.

Tyler emerged from the back, his costume long gone. Gloria scooted over and wrapped her arms around her grandson. "You were magnificent, Tyler."

Tyler swiped at his cowlick and smiled. "Thanks, Grams."

Gloria stayed for a few more minutes chatting with her family before she made her way out to her car and headed home.

The evening had been just what the doctor ordered and Gloria was thankful for not only her wonderful family, but also a diversion from her own situation.

Now all she had to do was get inside the police station with Margaret and try to figure out who had set Paul up!

***

Margaret pushed the cleaning cart to the end of the hall and stopped in front of an open door. "We have to empty trash cans? Every single one?"

Gloria nodded. "Yeah. There can't be many," she said.

Margaret scrunched her nose and stared down the long hall. "You're kidding."

Gloria followed her gaze. There were quite a few offices...but it was only emptying office wastebaskets. How bad could it be? It wasn't like cleaning out a restaurant dumpster.

Margaret reached for a pair of rubber gloves and slipped them on. She stepped inside the nearest office and looked around. "No wastebasket in here." She turned to go.

"Did you check under the desk?" Gloria asked.

"No. Why would someone put a wastebasket underneath the desk?"

Gloria leveled her gaze.

Margaret rolled her eyes. "All right. I'll check!" She stomped across the room, yanked the chair away from the desk and bent over as she peeked under the desk.

She reached under the desk and pulled out an overflowing wastebasket. "Well, if that isn't the stupidest place to put your trash," she mumbled.

She carried the wastebasket over to the cart, opened the large garbage bag and dumped the contents inside. She stomped back over to the desk and gave the empty wastebasket a heave-ho as she tossed it underneath.

"Margaret," Gloria warned.

"All *right!*" Margaret reached under the desk, set the empty wastebasket upright and slid the chair back in place.

Margaret grumbled about emptying the trash in the second office so Gloria told her they would switch tasks and she would empty the wastebaskets while Margaret spot swept the floors.

When they got to Captain Davies' office, Gloria picked up his wastebasket and peeked inside. She glanced at Margaret. "You keep an eye out. I want to sift through his trash for clues."

Margaret nodded and headed for the door.

Gloria carefully inspected each of the crumpled pieces of paper inside the basket before tossing them into the large garbage bag. One could tell a lot about a person by examining their trash.

Several slips of paper were pink pad messages from the receptionist. One was a message, telling Captain Davies to call his wife. Another was from someone named Fred in the homicide division. A third was from a drycleaner, telling him his uniform was ready for pick up. The fourth and final message Gloria found inside the wastebasket was from Cal Evergreen, City Commissioner.

The same Cal Evergreen who had solicited a "lady" of the night and supposedly been one of the unfortunate victims Paul was blackmailing. Gloria would bet money the commissioner was strong-arming the captain to fire Paul.

The only other items inside the wastebasket were an empty fast food bag, a drink cup, junk mail and several wads of chewed gum stuck to the sides of the bin.

Gloria scraped as much of the gum from the sides of the basket as she could and then tossed the chewed chunks in the trash bag.

Margaret, still standing outside guarding the door, wrinkled her nose. "That's disgusting."

"I agree."

The girls made quick work of the light cleaning. When they reached the end of the hall, they noticed an employee breakroom.

Gloria peeked in through the glass windowpane. Kim had given her a list of duties and Gloria pulled the sheet of paper from her pocket as she scanned the list.

"Employee breakroom. Empty trash, wipe inside of microwave, unload dishwasher, spot sweep the floor."

Gloria grasped the door handled, twisted the knob and stepped inside. The room was empty.

Gloria held the door while Margaret pushed the cleaning cart into the room.

Gloria handed the list to Margaret. "I'll let you pick out what you want to do."

Margaret glanced at the list and handed it back. "None of the above."

"Margaret…"

"Okay! I'll empty the dishwasher." Margaret opened the dishwasher and pulled out a cup while Gloria stepped over to the tall trashcan beside the vending machine.

She leaned over the top and looked inside. It was loaded with wadded up food wrappers, half-eaten fruit and discarded soda cans.

There was no way she was going to dig through the trash. Instead, she lifted the whole bag out, tied the top in a knot and dumped it into the larger garbage bag attached to the cleaning cart.

She opened the cupboards beneath the sink, reached inside for a sponge and then turned the faucet on. Gloria wet the sponge and began wiping the inside of the microwave.

They made quick work of the list of duties and moved on. The only rooms left to clean were the restrooms...and the locker rooms.

Gloria stopped the cart in front of the restrooms. The women's restroom was on the left, the men's on the right. "Should we divide and conquer?" That was what Gloria had in mind, but not Margaret.

"Nope. We work together. I clean sinks and you clean..."

"Toilets," Gloria guessed.

Margaret nodded. "You know I have a weak stomach."

It was true. Margaret had a strong gag reflex. Ruth had the same problem.

Gloria relented. "Okay."

After all, Margaret had been kind enough to agree to come along on this unorthodox fact finding mission, with a little persuasion. Well, a lot of persuasion...but the result was all that mattered...she was here.

Margaret held the women's restroom door and Gloria pushed the cart inside. The room was larger than Gloria thought it would be. The walls were floor-to-ceiling pink tile. They matched the floor, which was the same pale pink tile.

The room consisted of a row of sinks, three standard-size toilet stalls and one handicapped stall.

Margaret grabbed the glass cleaner and sprayed each of the mirrors hanging above the sinks. Next, she tore off paper towels and began wiping the mirrors clean.

Gloria headed to the stall on the left. She took a deep breath, pushed the door open and looked inside. It was as clean as could be expected. She squeezed a generous amount of toilet bowl cleaner in the first toilet bowl and moved onto the second one.

All three stalls were in good shape and needed only a light cleaning. Gloria should have known it was too good to be true.

When she reached the handicapped stall on the end, she pushed the door open and stepped inside. It was a mess. Someone had taken rolls of toilet paper and "teepeed" the inside. The sink, the hand dryer and the toilet. Not only that, they had emptied the wastebasket on the floor.

Gloria swallowed hard and cast an uneasy glance at the toilet.

Margaret wandered over and looked inside the stall. "The toilet paper exploded?"

"Here, let me help." Margaret grabbed a handful of the tissue from the wall-mounted dryer.

Gloria approached the toilet and her heart sank when she looked inside the bowl. The prankster had filled the entire bowl with wads of tissue and she could tell by looking at it, the toilet was clogged.

She glanced at Margaret. "You best move back to sink duty. This isn't going to be pretty."

Margaret's face paled and she nodded. "Good luck."

Gloria positioned a clean, empty garbage bag near the toilet and with one gloved hand, scooped piles of sopping wet paper into the plastic bag.

After she cleared the bowl, she lifted one leg, stuck her foot on the handle and flushed the toilet, all the while praying it would go down.

"Whoosh!"

She opened her eyes. The toilet bowl was clean and full of clear water. Gloria tied a knot in the top of the garbage bag, peeled her gloves off and headed for the door. "I'm going to take this out to the dumpster."

Margaret nodded. "You want me to go with you?"

The dumpster was in the back of the building and Kim had shown her the door before she headed over to the jail, attached to the other end of the police station.

"Nope. I can handle it." Gloria headed down the hall. When she reached the rear exit door, she pushed down on the bar with the tips of her elbows.

She backed out of the building and noticed there was a keypad above the handle on the outside of the door. She frowned. Kim hadn't mentioned a code to get back in.

Gloria reached out and grabbed the door right before it closed. She knelt down, grabbed a small

nearby rock and wedged the rock between the door
and the jamb.

Secure in the knowledge she wasn't going to get
locked out, Gloria stepped into the brisk evening air.
The smell of grilling burgers wafted in the air and
Gloria's stomach grumbled.

She turned her attention to the dumpster off to the
side. It was directly under a bright street light.
Gloria shifted her gaze to the fence near the back and
picked up the pace as she carried her bag of trash to
the green dumpster.

She lifted the dumpster lid, swung the bag over her
head and tossed it into the bin. Gloria dropped the
lid and headed for the door.

A movement off to one side caught Gloria's
attention. It was a police cruiser, its engine running.
Pulled up alongside the cop car was another vehicle,
the high beam headlights shining right on her.

Gloria couldn't tell what kind of vehicle it was, but
she did notice two things: The second vehicle was
dark. On the front of the vehicle was a yellow,
government issued plate.

Her eyes squinted and she glanced at the plate's ID. There was a set of numbers. After the numbers were the letters "DED." Gloria kicked the small rock from the door, stepped inside and pulled the door shut. "DED, DED," she whispered under her breath.

She picked up the pace and hustled down the hall. Gloria pushed the women's restroom door open.

Margaret jumped and then clutched her chest. "You scared me half to death!"

"DED," Gloria said.

Margaret's eyes widened. "DED? You mean someone is dead?"

Chapter 10

"No!" Gloria leaned against the door and shook her head. "When I was taking out the trash, I noticed a cop car parked out back. Parked alongside the cop car was a dark sedan with a yellow license plate. It was the kind of plates used on government-owned vehicles. The headlights were right on me so I had to look quick."

She went on. "The license plate. It was three numbers, followed by three letters, "DED."

Margaret stuck her hand on her hip. "I think I can remember DED."

Gloria nodded. "Me too.

The girls finished cleaning the women's restroom and wandered into the adjoining women's locker room.

The room was large. Several long, low benches ran through the center. Along the walls were tall but narrow metal lockers. On the other end of the room were the showers. The shower area consisted of one large, open shower with two smaller, private shower stalls off to the side.

It reminded Gloria of the locker and shower rooms they had back in high school where all the girls showered at the same time. It wasn't a pleasant experience when she was in grade school. She couldn't imagine showering in a large, open area as an adult!

Gloria pulled out her handy dandy "Kim" list and searched for locker room instructions. "The only thing we need to do in here is make sure the dirty towels are in the towel hamper and there are no empty shampoo bottles or trash."

Margaret tossed a couple wet towels in the towel hamper while Gloria tiptoed to the showers to make sure the stalls were clean.

After everything was spic and span, they headed back out into the hall.

Gloria faced the men's restroom. She took a deep breath and placed both hands on the outer door. "Ready for this?"

Margaret drew herself up to her full 4' 8" frame and squared her shoulders. "Ready as I'll ever be."

Gloria held the door while Margaret pushed the cart inside. The men's restroom was larger than the women's, probably because there were more men on the police force than women.

Margaret eyed the urinals with disgust. "Ugh."

Gloria followed her gaze. "Don't worry, Margaret. I'll take care of these if you clean the sinks and mirrors."

The girls got to work. Gloria was anxious to finish this task so they could move on to the locker room. She still wasn't sure what, if anything, she would find inside but at least this way she could say she left no stone unturned.

When the girls finished cleaning the bathroom, Gloria pushed the cleaning cart into the men's locker room and off to the side.

The layout was similar to the women's locker room, except this room was even larger. There was also a large, metal locker tucked away in the corner.

Gloria's radar went up. She stepped over to the locker and studied the outside. The smaller lockers were numbered. This one was marked "Authorized

Personnel Only." She wondered whom that "authorized personnel" was.

Gloria rattled the handle. It was locked. Gloria kicked the bottom with the tip of her tennis shoe. "I wish I knew what was in there."

The locker sat atop a wooden pallet. Under the pallet was open space. Margaret pointed at the open space. "Dare ya to stick your hand in there."

"Uh-uh. I doubt it has ever been cleaned." Gloria shuddered as she envisioned a furry rodent nibbling on her fingertips.

Next to the locker was a small handle. "I wonder what this is for." Gloria grasped the handle and pushed. It was some sort of walk-in closet. She ran her hand along the wall in search of a light switch.

There was no switch so she swatted at the ceiling as she blindly searched for a string. Her hand made contact with a small string. Gloria tugged on the dangling cord and bright light flooded the space. It was a supply closet full of clean towels, bars of soap, men's body wash and shampoo.

Gloria lifted towels and peeked behind the tidy rows of sundries.

Margaret lifted her gaze. "The women's locker room didn't have this," she commented.

It was true. There was no extra closet full of goodies.

A sudden noise caught Margaret's attention. "Did you hear that?" she whispered.

Gloria nodded. "Yeah. Sounds like someone is in the bathroom."

"Did you put the 'closed for cleaning' sign in front of the door?" Gloria asked.

Margaret shook her head. "I didn't know I was supposed to."

The echo of someone whistling filled the locker room. "Oh no! Someone is coming!"

Gloria peeked around the corner of the closet and caught a glimpse of a man, naked as a jaybird and holding a towel.

She shoved Margaret inside the closet and yanked the door shut. She held a finger to her lips.

The whistling continued and even picked up pace. Through the crack in the door, Gloria watched as the man hung his towel on a hook. He sauntered into a shower stall and pulled the curtain shut. "We should make a run for it."

"How will we get the cleaning cart out?" Margaret mumbled.

Gloria frowned. There was no way they could make it out without drawing attention to their presence. "I guess we will have to wait for him to leave."

Margaret nudged forward. "Can you see anything?"

The only thing visible was the towel and the shower curtain. Gloria squeezed her eyes shut and prayed he would hurry up. The man was in no hurry as he took his sweet old time.

Gloria's foot cramped. She lifted her leg and shook her foot, kicking Margaret in the shin in the process.

"Ouch!"

"Shh!"

"Stop kicking me," Margaret hissed.

Finally, the man emerged, grabbed the towel from the hook, wrapped it around his body and stepped over to the lockers.

It seemed like an eternity before the young cop finished changing into street clothes. He rolled up his uniform, shoved it in his duffel bag and strolled out of the locker room.

He turned the lights off on his way out.

When the outer door closed, Gloria swung the closet door open. "Let's get out of here before anyone else shows up."

Using the light from the closet as a guide, Gloria made her way across the room. She flipped the main light switch back on, reached for the cart and pulled it toward the exit. When they were safely out in the hall, she turned to Margaret. "Did you see anything?"

Margaret stiffened her back. "I'm a married woman, Gloria Rutherford! Of course I didn't see anything!"

Gloria rolled her eyes. "Not the nudist...a clue!"

"Oh." Margaret shook her head. "Nope."

The girls pushed the cleaning cart to the supply room in the back, carried two large garbage bags full of trash to the dumpster and headed out to search for Kim.

The night wasn't a total loss. Commissioner Cal Evergreen was in contact with Captain Davies. Gloria guessed it had something to do with Paul.

There was also the government vehicle parked alongside the cop car, after hours, in the back of the station. Why there? Why after hours?

Gloria swung by a fast food restaurant before heading toward Belhaven. The girls ate in the car and discussed the case.

"What's the next step?" Margaret asked.

Gloria needed to do a little research, try to find out who owned a license plate with "DED." She hoped that perhaps Joe would be able to tell her who had worked tonight's evening shift.

Gloria also planned to do a little research on the suspects, although it was tough finding anything on cops. Their home addresses, their spouse's names, anything. Paul would know, but Paul was MIA.

Well, sort of MIA. He was in Lansing doing who knew what.

Gloria dropped Margaret off at her house. She backed out of the drive and headed toward the farm.

She pulled Annabelle into the garage, climbed out of the car and exited through the side service door.

She had remembered to leave the porch light on and it was a good thing.

A thin layer of snow covered the deck. She unlocked the back door, tossed her purse on the chair and held the door for Mally.

Mally raced out the door and darted past Gloria. She was growing accustomed to the snow and frolicked around in the fluffy white stuff while Gloria shoveled the fresh layer of snow off the porch, the steps and the sidewalk.

Gloria frowned as she thought about her children's upcoming visit. She still hadn't told any of them the wedding might be delayed, hoping against hope she could somehow figure out who was setting Paul up so they could move forward with the wedding.

The case was harder to crack than she thought. The biggest obstacle was getting close to the suspects. She knew so little about any of them.

Gloria thunked the snow off the shovel and propped it against the wall in the corner of the porch.

Inside the house, she unbuttoned her jacket, hung it and her scarf on the hook, placed her wet boots in the boot tray and headed for the computer.

She might not be able to find out much about the police who worked at the station, but she could do a little digging into the Verona family. Mitzi Verona was a colorful character and always seemed to pop up in the news with some antic either she or her offspring was involved in.

Gloria eased into the desk chair and turned the computer on. Puddles waited for Gloria to settle in before he jumped onto her lap and curled up.

Gloria pet Puddles while she checked her email and then the local weather. Tomorrow's forecast was only a few flurries but the day after was shaping up to be a doozy, with forecasters predicting blizzard-like conditions.

When she finished checking the weather, she typed in Mitzi Verona. A picture of Mitzi, wearing a black and white ballroom gown and holding a glittery gold mask to her face popped up first.

Gloria enlarged the picture and studied the woman's facial features. A twinkle of mischief sparkled in her sharp blue eyes. Mitzi looked as if she had a secret she was keeping.

Several articles described Mitzi's love for her family and furry pets. She owned a large horse farm in Rapid Creek and split her time between the horse farm and a large estate in East Grand Rapids, the tonier part of the city.

Mitzi was one of two people who had received Paul's extortion note. From what she had heard, Paul had contacted her directly. She remembered Minnie telling her there were even more victims, yet to be named.

Gloria drummed her fingers on the desktop. She wondered how hard it would be to approach the wealthy socialite.

Gloria had reached a dead end. Other than track Paul down and demand he let her help in the investigation, she was running out of options. Gloria's pride wouldn't allow her to approach Paul.

He was the one threatening to call off the wedding. He was the one who left town without telling her where he was going, although he had called but didn't bother leaving a message.

Gloria quickly searched "Verona, Rapid Creek, Michigan." A picture popped up. It was a beautiful horse farm with rolling hills. Off in the distance, a magnificent home sat perched high atop a hill. She tried several different searches to track down an address.

"Now what?" she asked Puddles. Puddles opened one eye and yawned sleepily.

Gloria set Puddles on the chair and shuffled to the kitchen. She filled a teacup with water and popped it into the microwave. While the water warmed, Gloria paced the kitchen floor. If only she could talk to Mitzi Verona, explain her situation. First, she had to find her.

The microwave beeped. Gloria carefully lifted the steaming water from the microwave, dunked a teabag in the cup and swirled it around.

A thought popped into Gloria's head. The property appraiser! That was how she could locate the address to Mitzi's horse farm!

Gloria scurried into the dining room and once again settled in front of the computer. She pulled up the county property appraiser's website and typed in Verona. Page after page of people named Verona popped up. Gloria had no idea there were so many.

She narrowed her search and typed in "M Verona." Still nothing. Maybe the property was under Percival Verona, Mitzi's deceased husband.

Gloria typed a "P" in front of Verona and voila! Percival Verona's name appeared.

Gloria clicked on the link and an address in Rapid Creek popped up. Gloria grabbed her yellow pad, jotted the address down and set the pen on top.

She typed Mitzi Verona's name inside the search bar again and read several articles about the wealthy matriarch. Although she spent most of her winters in

East Grand Rapids, she visited her beloved horses at least once a week and, in fact, was hosting a large animal shelter fundraiser that upcoming weekend.

"We are in the midst of preparations for this gala event and I am spending more time at the horse farm than I normally do during the winter months," she told the reporter.

Gloria glanced at the article's date. It was published three days ago, which meant there was a good chance Mitzi Verona was still at her horse farm, which meant Gloria was going to visit the horse farm the next morning.

Gloria was so focused on her investigation; she nearly jumped out of her skin when her cell phone chirped. She glanced down at the screen. It was Andrea.

She lifted the phone and pressed the "answer" button. "Hello dear."

"Hi Gloria. I'm calling to check in. You know, make sure everything is all right."

Gloria smiled. "Make sure I didn't pack my bags and flee to Florida?"

Andrea laughed. "Something like that."

"Nah. I was being silly," Gloria sighed. She glanced at Mitzi Verona's picture on the screen. "What are you doing tomorrow morning?"

"Nothing much. You need a sidekick?"

Gloria shifted the mouse back and forth. "Maybe. You ever heard of Mitzi Verona?"

"Who hasn't?"

"Well, it appears she was one of the individuals caught up in the extortion plot."

She went on. "It seems Mrs. Verona would be the most approachable and since I think she's staying at her horse farm in Rapid Creek, I thought we could make a run by there."

"What excuse will you use?" Andrea asked.

"The perfect excuse," Gloria said. "She's hosting an animal shelter fundraiser this weekend. Apparently, she's a big animal lover, which means our excuse will be..."

"At Your Service!" Andrea exclaimed. "Perfect! Maybe we can talk to her about helping us. Not only does she have a lot of money, she has a lot of connections."

"Kill two birds with one stone," Gloria said.

The two agreed Andrea would swing by around eight the following morning to pick Gloria up. They would stop by Dot's Restaurant for breakfast and then head over to the Verona horse farm.

For the first time since Paul had mentioned postponing the wedding, Gloria felt like they had a real shot at finally getting somewhere and maybe she wasn't "spinning her wheels."

Gloria climbed into bed a short while later. Mally settled into her doggie bed in the corner and Puddles took his usual spot near the head of the bed.

Gloria pulled the covers around her neck, closed her eyes and prayed a simple prayer. "Please God. Help me solve this mystery and bring Paul home."

Chapter 11

Andrea was right on time and Gloria was waiting
for her at the door. Gloria had tossed and turned the
entire night hoping Mitzi Verona held a clue that
would somehow unlock the mystery of who was trying
to incriminate Paul.

When they reached town, Andrea slowed in front
of Dot's Restaurant and pulled into an empty spot out
front.

Gloria tucked her scarf around her neck and slid
out of the passenger seat. The wind had picked up
and sent blasts of cold air that pierced through the
collar of her jacket. She wasn't ready for old man
winter yet.

The girls slipped inside the restaurant, stomped
the snow off their boots and headed to a table in the
back.

Dot darted behind the lattice that separated the
dining room from the back. She smiled when she
caught a glimpse of Andrea and Gloria. She met them
at the table, coffee pot in hand. "What are you two up
to today?"

Gloria turned her empty coffee cup right side up and slid it across the table as she waited for Dot to fill the cup. "We're heading over to Mitzi Verona's farm."

Dot filled Gloria's cup. Next, she filled Andrea's cup and set it in front of her. "The wealthy gal with the enormous horse farm over near Rapid Creek?"

Gloria nodded. "Yep. She is one of the people Paul 'supposedly' tried to extort money. We're hoping she might have a clue to the real culprit."

Dot shifted the pot to her other hand. "I heard she's a real firecracker."

Gloria had heard the same thing, that the woman was a real character. It didn't make her a bad person, though. It definitely made her more...interesting.

Gloria was never one to shy away from a challenge so that didn't bother her in the least.

Andrea reached for the breakfast menu. "We're hungry."

"Pancakes sound good," Gloria decided. "That and maybe some bacon."

Dot pulled her notepad from her apron and jotted Gloria's order on the pad. She turned to Andrea. "What about you young lady?"

Andrea flipped the menu over. "Western omelet, rye toast and a side of sausage links." She closed the menu and shoved it back in the center slot.

Dot wrote Andrea's order on a second slip of paper. "I always wondered what the inside of her fancy horse farm looked like."

"If we weasel our way inside, I'll try to snap a few pictures," Gloria teased.

Dot snorted. "I don't doubt that you will." She headed to the kitchen to place the girls' order and Gloria turned her attention to the other diners. She recognized most of them, including Judith Arnett, who sat in a booth with a couple of her cronies.

Gloria gave her a small wave and Judith winked. The archenemy phase was finally over and the two women were more or less frenemies now...maybe even friends.

Judith had helped with Ruth's case and most recently, when Lucy was in trouble. She wouldn't call

Judith salt-of-the-earth, but the woman had redeeming qualities. Being loyal to her friends was at the top of the list.

The girls' breakfast arrived and while they ate, they discussed the case. Gloria still firmly believed someone inside the Montbay Sheriff's Station was involved in the extortion or knew someone who was involved.

She thought about Cal Evergreen, City Commissioner. She wondered if there was a way she could approach him to ask him some questions. She had heard rumors he was a hard man and rude to boot.

How could a public figure be so unlikeable yet still keep getting re-elected? Unless, of course, he had connections, which wouldn't surprise Gloria. She believed some people who held government positions got to where they were by greasing someone's palm.

After they finished eating, Gloria slipped her jacket on and headed to the cash register. Andrea was right behind her.

Gloria handed Dot her ticket and debit card. She swiped the card and handed it back. "Let me know what you find out," Dot said.

Gloria shifted to the side so Andrea could pay. "We can stop back by if you want," Gloria offered.

Andrea handed Dot a twenty-dollar bill. Dot rang up Andrea's meal, opened the cash register and counted out her change. "Sure. I'm dying to know how the upper echelon squeak by."

The girls climbed into the truck, backed out of the parking spot and headed for Sunshine Stables.

Mitzi's horse farm was not in Rapid Creek, but rather just north of Rapid Creek, halfway between Rapid Creek and Green Springs to be precise.

Gloria had passed by the farm plenty of times and wondered who owned such a palatial place in the country. Now she knew.

A six-foot tall wrought iron fence with iron finials tips surrounded the palatial estate. Two large gates stood sentinel at the end of the drive. The massive gates were wide open.

Andrea stopped the truck near the gate. There was a callbox on a post outside the gate. She rolled down the window and stuck her head out. "Hello?"

No one answered and she tried again. Nothing. She turned to Gloria. "What should I do?"

"Drive through."

Andrea took her foot off the brake and gently pushed on the gas pedal.

The paved drive was long and winding. Majestic Michigan maple trees lined the drive. Gloria could envision how beautiful it would be in the fall when the leaves were changing color.

They rounded a curve and Gloria gasped. Although the estate was visible from the main road, the sheer size of it up close was stunning. It was a large, two-story with a wraparound porch. The exterior of the home was a mixture of fieldstone and some other type of stone Gloria didn't recognize.

Attached to the right of the main structure was a long, single story addition. The side that faced the road was a wall of windows and Gloria caught a glimpse of what appeared to be a pool inside. To the

143

left of the main structure was a five-car attached garage.

The drive forked off and beyond that, she caught a glimpse of a large horse barn, which matched the house. A maze of fences jutted out and around the barn and then disappeared over a towering hill.

In front of the horse barn was another building. This one was much smaller. "Let's try over there," Gloria suggested.

Andrea veered to the right and parked in front of the small building. In front of the building was a covered porch and under the porch was a swing. Sitting in the swing was a man. He eyed them with interest as they climbed out of the truck.

He slowly eased out of the swing and clomped over in his cowboy boots, shoved one hand in the pocket of his bib overalls and tipped his cowboy hat. "Hello ladies. Welcome to Sunshine Stables. How can I help you?"

Andrea followed Gloria onto the porch and stopped next to her. "We are looking for Mitzi Verona. We heard she might be here today," Andrea explained.

The young man, who couldn't have been a day over 21, swiped the hair out of his eyes and lowered his hat. "Yep. Mrs. Verona is here. She's..."

"Whoa Nellie!" Out of nowhere, a horse and rider galloped past them, the horse's hooves clattered loudly on the cement walkway as they zipped by.

The horse was moving so fast, Gloria was only able to catch a brief glimpse of the rider and the rider's shocking white hair, which contrasted against a black helmet and black riding boots that reached the rider's knees.

Three heads turned to watch the horse and rider as they bolted up the hill and disappeared over the other side. "There she goes."

The young man turned his attention to Andrea and Gloria. "She'll be back. She's trying to break in Sassy," he explained as he shook his head. "She's a wild one."

Gloria wasn't certain if he was referring to the horse – or the rider.

He extended his hand. "I'm Chad Stetson, ranch hand and Mrs. Verona's right hand man."

Gloria took his hand. His grip was warm and friendly. She immediately got a good feel from him. "Gloria Rutherford."

He shook Andrea's hand next, a little too long in Gloria's opinion. "Andrea Malone."

He reluctantly released Andrea's hand. "Is there something I can help you with?"

"I know Mrs. Verona is a generous donor to a variety of projects near and dear to her heart," Gloria said. "We know of one not far from here. It's a small start-up. We would be thrilled if she could spare a few minutes to offer advice...or if she might be willing to help."

Chad nodded. "Yeah. She has a heart of gold and a soft spot for her furry friends." He waved them along as he made his way to the side door of the large horse barn. "What kind of project?" he asked.

"It's a new training center for service dogs over in Green Springs. 'At Your Service' is the name. Like Gloria said, they're starting up and could use some backing," Andrea explained.

Chad opened the service door and stepped to the side to let Andrea and Gloria in. "She has her hands full right now with the large fundraiser this weekend but I'm sure she'll have a minute to chat."

The trio wandered down the side of the stalls and Gloria peeked at some of the majestic horses inside. On the outside of each of the stalls was a plaque with the horses' names. "Buck, Daisy, Gypsy..."

They passed by the stalls and exited through the open doors on the other end of the barn.

Mrs. Verona and Sassy had returned from their run and were now trotting around the fenced area on the backside of the barn. She waved when she caught a glimpse of Chad, Andrea and Gloria.

Mrs. Verona tugged on the reins, and horse and rider trotted over.

Mitzi Verona shielded her eyes and stared down at the trio. "Sassy is going to be the death of me yet," she groaned as she eased her boot from the stirrup and swung her leg over the side of the horse. She jumped to the ground and handed the reins to Chad.

Chad opened the gate and led Sassy and the women back toward the horse barn.

Mitzi's bright blue eyes honed in on Gloria. Not one for small talk, Mitzi Verona spoke her mind. She pointed at Gloria. "Say, you look familiar." She pinched the tip of her riding glove and tugged on the end.

Gloria frowned. She had never laid eyes on Mitzi Verona in her life before today. Gloria was certain she had never attended one of Mitzi's highfalutin shindigs.

Mitzi pulled the other glove off and whacked the soft leather against the palm of her hand. "I know! You're the lady who goes around solving mysteries." She tapped the side of her chin with her finger. "Wasn't there some bank robber whose body was found in an old, abandoned house not far from here?"

Gloria glanced at Andrea out of the corner of her eye. Mitzi was talking about the time they found Arthur Goldstone's body in Andrea's shed.

Mitzi answered her own question. "Yeah. That was it."

148

Her bright blue eyes widened. "Then there was something about some crazy lady who chained herself to the front of a restaurant." She must have been talking about Frances, her sister Liz's friend, who went a little cuckoo when her beloved Milt disappeared.

They stepped inside the stable and watched as Chad brushed Sassy with a tan dandy brush. Sassy loved the attention and nuzzled Chad's arm.

Mitzi stepped over to a wooden box anchored to the side of a tall, wooden post. She reached inside the box and pulled out a sugar cube. She extended her hand toward Sassy who leaned over and gobbled the sweet treat while Mitzi patted her nose.

She slid a sideways glance. "Someone is trying to blackmail me and my family."

Gloria shuffled her feet and nodded. "That is one of the reasons we're here."

Mitzi abruptly turned on her heel and motioned them to follow. "Let's go inside the house."

The women crossed the drive and passed the massive garage. They picked up the pace as they strolled across the tiered wooden deck toward a slider door on the side of the house.

Mitzi slid the slider door open and led them into a large mudroom. The mudroom was larger than Gloria's entire kitchen. Lined up against one whole wall were cubbies. Under each cubby were hooks.

Mitzi plopped down on a bench and tugged on the heel of her riding boot. She set both boots next to the bench, shrugged out of her riding jacket and hung it on a hook nearby.

"You said someone blackmailing me and my family was one of the reasons you were here," She unclipped the strap that fastened her riding helmet, slipped it off her head and slid it inside the cubby directly above her jacket. Her pure white cropped hair stood straight up on her head.

Gloria grinned.

Mitzi returned the smile and lifted her hand. "What? It's standing straight up, isn't it?"

Mitzi ran her hands through her hair. "So what's the other reason? Money? Charity?"

Andrea stepped closer. "We know you have pet projects and are a huge supporter of animal charities."

"And?" Mitzi prompted.

"We know of a small kennel in Green Springs. Most recently, it was a puppy mill but the owners are trying to turn it around...turn it into a training center for service dogs."

"Along with a boarding kennel," Gloria added.

Mitzi nodded. "Hmmm...sounds intriguing. I've looked into supporting service dogs training but never gotten personally involved in one of their projects."

She crossed the mudroom and headed for a set of French doors at the other end.

Andrea and Gloria followed her lead.

Mitzi swung the doors open and Gloria and Andrea stepped into the kitchen.

Gloria sucked in a breath. It looked like it belonged in a French chateau. Large hand-hewn beams crisscrossed the ceiling. Twinkling vintage glass pendant lights hung over the expansive quartz island. Nestled inside the quartz counters was a copper farmhouse sink. The sink overlooked a fenced courtyard.

Custom antique white cabinets filled an entire wall. Tucked in the corners were small nooks and crannies, perfect for stuffing odds and ends inside.

"Have a seat," Mitzi nodded to the wooden barstools tucked under the massive center island. "Would you care for tea or hot cocoa perhaps?"

Gloria shook her head. "No thanks."

"I will take a cup of tea," Andrea said, figuring that if she drank it slowly, it would buy them more time.

Gloria changed her mind. "I guess I'll have a cup, if you don't mind."

Mitzi glanced over her shoulder. "Of course not."

She lifted a silver teakettle from the stove, filled it with water, turned the gas burner on high and set the pot on top.

She reached inside the cupboard and pulled out three fluted bone teacups trimmed in gold. They looked fragile...and very expensive.

Gloria knew a little about fine bone china. "Those look like Aynsley." Aynsley was a British manufacturer. The company created delicate works of collectible china.

Mitzi smiled. "Good eye. Yes. These are Aynsley. I have several collections." She set the saucer and teacup in front of Gloria. She set another saucer and cup in front of Andrea.

She placed clear tea bags in each of the cups. "I hope you like vanilla."

Gloria loved vanilla. "It sounds perfect." The tea bags were almost as lavish as the cups.

The kettle whistled and Mitzi carefully poured piping hot water into each of the cups. The rich aroma of vanilla filled the air.

She placed the kettle back on the stove and settled into a barstool on the end. Mitzi lifted her cup and sipped her tea. "I am interested in helping the service dogs. Perhaps one day soon, after my party, I can

153

visit this 'At Your Service' dog training facility to see what can be done."

It was wonderful news...an unexpected bonus.

"Now let's discuss the other." She gazed at them shrewdly. "The real reason you are here."

Chapter 12

Gloria poured out her story of how she believed someone had set Paul up. She explained that she had compiled a list of suspects who had it in for Paul and even told Mitzi how she had noticed a government plate on a car parked behind the police station the previous evening.

"What were you doing at the police station?" Mitzi asked.

Gloria dropped her eyes to her cup and fiddled with the handle. "Working undercover."

Andrea grinned. "As a cleaning lady."

"Sounds intriguing." Mitzi laughed. "You're my kinda gal." She listened intently as Gloria continued her story.

When Gloria got to the part where Paul was MIA and the wedding tentatively postponed, the woman reached out and touched Gloria's hand. "My dear. I am so sorry to hear that. Why, my own Percival and I were married forty years before he passed away last year." Her eyes clouded over.

"I'm sorry," Gloria said. At least Paul was still alive...she hoped.

Mitzi swallowed the last of tea in her cup and lifted it. "More?" She refilled the empty cups and dunked her teabag in her cup. "There is more to the story the public doesn't know about."

Gloria's heart skipped a beat. This was it...this was what she had been waiting for.

"Two days ago, I received another demand for money. This time, it was much more than the piddly fifty grand." Mitzi sucked in a breath. "The note demanded two hundred-fifty thousand dollars."

Andrea's mouth dropped open. "Holy smokes!"

Mitzi nodded. "Holy smokes is right. I can pay the amount but where will it end?"

Mitzi had a point. Whoever was extorting her had no intention of stopping. In fact, Gloria had a sneaky suspicion this was just the beginning.

"What could they possibly have on you?" The online illegal gambling story had made headlines. There was nothing left to reveal.

Mitzi lowered her head, her lips drawn in a thin line. She was about to drop a bombshell. Gloria could feel it. Something so big, Mitzi was willing to pay a whole lot of money for someone to keep quiet.

She looked up, her blue eyes staring straight into Gloria's. "I. My." She sucked in a breath and closed her eyes. "I gave my firstborn, my oldest son, up for adoption."

She went on. "Whoever sent me the note knows all about my son. He was born before I met Percival. My parents, we didn't have much money. In fact, we had no money. The baby needed so much I couldn't give but someone else...a loving family...could."

Mitzi spun the delicate cup in a circle on the saucer. "I...Percival knew about my son, but our other children, they don't...and I need to keep it that way."

"Does your son, the one you gave up...does he know who you are?" Andrea asked.

Mitzi shook her head. "No. Back then, they didn't have open adoptions like they do now. His adoptive parents were so concerned I would try to take him back, they moved. I had no idea where he was or if he was even still alive."

Mitzi's hand shook as she lifted the teacup to her lips. "Whoever is behind this extortion tracked my son down."

Gloria tapped her index finger on the counter. "Why not tell your children about their stepbrother?"

Mitzi's eyes widened. "They must never know. It would be as if they never knew their mother at all, like my whole life had been one big lie."

Gloria wasn't convinced. Maybe Mitzi had it all wrong and her grown children would welcome him with open arms. It was apparent Mitzi did not see it that way.

Mitzi stepped over to the antique wooden bench seat near the door, lifted a gray designer handbag from the bench seat and carried it back to the bar. She opened the handbag, reached inside and pulled out a manila envelope.

She slid the envelope across the counter. "This is what was sent to me."

Gloria picked the envelope up and flipped it over. She unfolded the flap, reached inside and pulled out the contents. Inside the envelope was a picture of a man, his features chiseled, his dark hair slicked back. A smile lifted the corner of his mouth, as if he were highly amused by something.

Gloria reached into her purse and slipped her reading glasses on. The man's eyes were his most striking feature. They were identical to Mitzi Verona's own eyes. Gloria peered at Mitzi over the rim of her glasses. "This is your son?"

Mitzi nodded. "Kenneth Templeton. He lives in Indianapolis." She pointed to the folded sheet of paper Gloria held in her hand. "Read the note."

Gloria unfolded the note. Andrea leaned over her shoulder:

Kenneth C. Templeton, 1512 Bellweather Drive, Indianapolis, IN. Born July 26th, 1962.

Below that was one sentence.

"Leave $255k in unmarked bills in your mailbox at Sunshine Estates on Friday, December 22nd before ten o'clock p.m."

That was the end of the note. There was no "PK" signature at the bottom.

Gloria folded the note, looked at the photo one more time and slid both back inside the envelope. "This should be easy. Stakeout the end of your drive and see who shows up."

Mitzi shook her head. "December 22nd is the night of my 'Black Tie & Tails' gala party. It's my biggest fundraiser event of the year. The event raises hundreds of thousands of dollars for a local animal shelter and I am the host."

Whoever had written the note knew Mitzi would have her hands full, people would be passing by the mailbox all evening long and it would be easy for someone to stop by the mailbox, reach inside and take an envelope full of money...

Andrea lifted the envelope and tapped the tip on the quartz counter. "Do you think whoever it is will attend the party?"

Mitzi frowned. "It's possible. The thought had crossed my mind. There will be many people here. The guest list includes local mayors, government officials and other philanthropists."

"What about security?" Gloria asked.

Mitzi nodded. "Yes, of course. I always hire off-duty police to work. I have oodles of irreplaceable artwork and other valuables."

That meant more than likely Montbay Sheriff's finest would be on hand! This was like the perfect scheme. The culprit planned to steal from the poor woman right from under her nose.

Mitzi stared thoughtfully out the window. "You think either someone attending the gala or working the gala is the blackmailer?"

Gloria followed Mitzi's gaze. "That's exactly what I think!"

Andrea could see the wheels spinning in Gloria's mind. "You're up to something, aren't you?"

December 22nd. It was only a couple days before Gloria's children were scheduled to arrive. Gloria would have her house full...and her hands full then. Still, she could probably squeeze in a little hands-on sting now.

She turned to Mitzi. "How much do you want to catch the person who is blackmailing you?"

Mitzi clenched her fists. "Why I'd give anything to wring their sorry neck!"

"I think I can help you get to the bottom of this," Gloria said. "You'll need to invite me and a few of my friends to your party."

Mitzi marched over to a desk in the corner, reached inside one of the drawers and pulled out a manila folder. She flipped the folder open and several invitations fell out and onto the desk. "How many do you need?"

Gloria silently counted: Andrea, Dot, Ruth, Lucy, Margaret and Gloria. "Six."

Mitzi counted out six invitations and carried those and the envelopes to the bar area. She quickly addressed the invitations, popped each into an individual envelope and sealed them shut.

Mitzi slid the small stack of invitations across the counter. "The party starts at five on the dot," she said.

Gloria reached for the invitations. "We'll be here by 4:30. What should we wear?"

"The theme is black and white. Cocktail dress or long formal for the ladies," Mitzi said.

Mitzi extended her hand. "If you can find out who is doing this, I will forever be in your debt."

Gloria took Mitzi's hand. "I'm doing this for both of us, Mitzi," she reminded her.

"True," Mitzi replied. "We should exchange cell phone numbers."

Gloria reached for her purse and pulled out her cell phone. She entered Mitzi's number in her phone and gave Mitzi hers to do the same.

Gloria and Andrea slid off the barstools and headed for the back door. They passed the small desk and Andrea had a sudden thought. "Do you have a copy of the guest list?"

Gloria frowned. Why hadn't she thought of that?

"Yes, of course. Good idea." Mitzi held up a finger and darted out of the room. She returned a few minutes later, list in hand. She handed it to Gloria. "My son, Kenneth, you won't…"

Gloria made a zipping motion across her lips. "Our lips are sealed. We won't breathe a word."

Andrea nodded. "Mums the word."

Mitzi walked them out to the truck and waited until they were safely inside.

Andrea rolled down the driver's side window. "I'll bet your son turned out to be a great guy."

Mitzi stared thoughtfully at Andrea and glanced over at Gloria. "I loved Kenneth with all my heart." Her eyes glittered with unshed tears. "I didn't want to give him up. I was young..."

Andrea reached out and touched her arm. "I'm sure he understands, Mitzi."

Mitzi nodded but Gloria wasn't sure the woman was convinced. She had no idea what she would have done if she had been in the same situation. Back in those days, it was rare for children to be born out of wedlock. They married, married young or gave the babies up.

"Don't be so hard on yourself, Mitzi," Gloria said. "You made a wise decision and the right one for Kenneth and you."

Mitzi nodded. "I know." Her shoulders slumped as she walked away. It was obvious the woman was burdened with decades of guilt over her decision. Gloria prayed someday Mitzi would find it somewhere inside to forgive herself. Sometimes that was the hardest thing to do. Forgive yourself.

***

On the drive back to Belhaven, Andrea and Gloria chatted about the party. Gloria had never been to a gala event. Andrea vaguely remembered going to one as a child when she lived in New York City with her parents. The things she remembered the most were the beautiful gowns and sparkling lights...it almost seemed like a magical world and she felt like Cinderella.

As she got older, Andrea avoided parties and social events like the plague. She felt they were pretentious and the people who threw the parties just wanted to show off.

Now that she was older, she realized some of the events could be useful and actually help a cause...a good cause, like 'At Your Service.'

Andrea approached the stop sign and glanced in both directions. "Maybe I should hold a fundraiser at my place for 'At Your Service.' I could invite the whole town, serve scrumptious little finger foods and champagne. Charge like $50 a pop." She was throwing numbers out there, not certain what it would take to pull off a profitable event.

Gloria nodded. "Great idea. We can get some ideas from Mitzi's party. We could hold a raffle and have people donate services or gift cards."

Andrea turned the corner and pulled onto the main road. "Dot could give away a dinner for two, Lucy could throw in some shooting lessons."

"Ruth could offer 24-hour surveillance," Gloria kidded.

All joking aside, it was a brilliant idea. "Let's get through Paul's crisis, the wedding, my kids' upcoming visit and the holidays and then we'll talk about it."

"Sounds good." Andrea slowed the truck as they passed the city limit sign. "We should call a meeting with the girls so we can give them their party invitations and go over a plan."

Gloria reached for her cell phone and sent text messages to each one to set up a meeting at Dot's at five o'clock, right after Ruth closed up shop at the post office.

Each of the girls texted back, asking how the meeting with Mitzi Verona had gone. Gloria told them she would give them the details when they met.

Gloria slipped the phone inside her purse and set her purse on the floor of the truck. "I don't have a thing to wear to this party," she said.

"Neither do I," Andrea replied. "I have an idea! Why don't we head over to the antique store, Trinkets and Treasures in Green Springs? They have some cool vintage clothes!"

Gloria was game. She had no other plans, except to ramble around the farm and feel sorry for herself. She thought about Paul and wondered if he was still in Lansing.

Later, when she was alone, she would go over the guest list Mitzi had given her. When her mind had cleared and there were no distractions.

Andrea drove straight through Belhaven and headed toward Green Springs.

Chapter 13

Downtown Green Springs was busy. Gloria correctly guessed it was bustling with holiday shoppers.

Andrea turned the truck on a side street and parked in the alley behind the Main Street shops. There were two vintage, antique shops on the main thoroughfare.

The girls made a beeline for the closest one, *A Moment in Time*.

Gloria hadn't been in the store in a long time. In fact, the last time she had been in the shop was when she had been investigating Daniel Malone's murder, Andrea's husband. She didn't mention it to Andrea as they made their way to the entrance. There was no reason to bring up painful memories, especially around the holidays.

Gloria glanced down at Andrea's ring finger and made a mental note to ask Brian when he planned to ask Andrea to marry him. The last time Gloria and Brian had chatted, he'd shown her the engagement ring he had purchased for Andrea.

Gloria frowned. She hoped he wasn't getting cold feet, like someone else she knew.

The bell above the door chimed as they stepped inside. The interior of the quaint store was crammed floor-to-ceiling with oddities and antiquities.

Andrea knew where she was going and headed for the back of the store. Gloria followed behind.

In the rear of the shop were racks of clothes. Hanging against the far wall were dresses and long gowns. The girls sifted through the racks and studied each of the outfits. The theme was black and white. Gloria thought she remembered the invitation 'suggested' black and white attire but she didn't want to stick out like a sore thumb.

She opened her purse and pulled out her invitation. On the front was the silhouette of a man in a black and white tuxedo.

"*Black Tie and Tails*

Gala Event."

Gloria flipped the card open:

"*When: Tuesday, December 22nd at 5:00 p.m.*

Where: Sunshine Stables & Estate, Rapid Creek, Michigan

At the very bottom, in very small print: *Black and white attire suggested.*

There was also an email address to RSVP but Mitzi already knew Gloria and her friends would be there.

She placed the invitation inside the envelope and shoved the envelope back inside her bag.

Andrea pulled a shimmering cocktail dress from the fray. The top half of the dress was white and the bottom half a solid black. Sewn into the neckline and around the hem of the dress were sparkly glass beads.

She darted into the one and only fitting room and popped out a short time later. She twirled around in a circle while Gloria studied the dress. It fit her perfectly and the price was right...only twenty-five bucks.

Gloria, on the other hand, had no such luck. "Maybe I should buy a black jacket and wear my wedding dress since it doesn't look like I'm getting married now," she grumbled.

Andrea popped her on the arm. "Bite your tongue. Of course you're getting married, even if I have to drive to Lansing, bring Paul back home and drag him to the altar."

The thought of dainty little Andrea dragging anyone, anywhere, especially someone as big as Paul, made her smile. It made Andrea smile too.

She grabbed Gloria's arm. "C'mon. Let's head over to Trinkets and Treasures. Maybe we'll find something over there."

Andrea paid for her dress. The girls stopped by the truck and Andrea dropped it onto the seat. The girls wandered back down Main Street to Trinkets and Treasures.

The inside of the shop was crammed full of treasures and a lot of the items looked like the same stuff they had for sale inside *A Moment in Time*.

Gloria stopped in front of a gold and brown Barbie® camper and peeked inside. Her daughter, Jill, had an identical camper growing up. It brought back sudden memories of the many times she had played Barbie® with her young daughter.

Next to the camper was a TinkerToy® construction set. The set reminded Gloria of her sons.

She followed Andrea to the side of the shop where there were racks of clothes. This shop had a bigger selection and soon, Andrea found several dresses and gowns she insisted Gloria try on.

Gloria tried several and grew discouraged until she reached the bottom of the heap. The last one she tried was a perfect fit. It was a cream-colored dress, strapless with a fitted top and flowing bottom. The dress came to just below Gloria's knees. A silky black bolero jacket fit snugly over the top.

The pieces were separate but it was if they had been made for one another. Gloria turned to one side and then the other. She examined the garments for rips, tears and other defects but there were none. She stepped from behind the curtain and twirled 'round so Andrea could critique.

Andrea clapped her hands. "Perfect! I love it."

Gloria had to admit she did, too. The girls had found it in the discount section for the bargain price of thirty dollars. It was something Gloria could see herself wearing more than once, perhaps even on her honeymoon. She draped the dress over her arm, grabbed the jacket and carried her purchases to the cash register.

The clerk rang up the dress and jacket and carefully slid them into a plastic shopping bag. She handed the bag to Gloria. The shopping trip had been a huge success!

By the time they rolled into Belhaven, it was already four o'clock. There was just enough time to stop by Gloria's place to drop off the dress and let Mally out for a run.

Gloria noticed a moving truck in front of the farmhouse across the road when they pulled in the drive.

Andrea shut off the engine and hopped out of the driver's seat. She glanced across the road. "The new neighbors are finally moving in."

The construction crews had been working almost 'round the clock the past few days and Gloria had stopped over to talk to the young couple who had bought the place. They told Gloria their plan was to move in in time to celebrate Christmas in their new home. It looked as if they barely made it under the wire.

"I'll have to whip up a housewarming gift and take it over once they get settled." Gloria closed the passenger door and shuffled to the porch. She could see Mally's head peeking out through the window.

Gloria opened the door and Mally darted out onto the porch and down the steps. She raced around the front of the barn and disappeared, reappearing a short time later on the other side.

She galloped past the garden and rounded the corner of the house.

It took a few moments for her to come barreling around the front yard and Gloria could only guess she stopped to harass the birds or the squirrels that were out front near the bird feeder.

Andrea kept an eye on Mally while Gloria carried the dress inside and hung it in her bedroom closet. She placed it next to her wedding dress and a sob caught in her throat when she touched her wedding dress.

Gloria forced the dress, and her wedding, from her mind. For now, she had to focus on the task at hand – clearing Paul's name!

Gloria stepped out onto the porch and Mally darted inside. She wasn't keen on the cold yet and she didn't dilly dally out in the yard like she did during the summer months.

Gloria fed Mally and Puddles and then headed back out. "I'll drive my car so you don't have to come back here," Gloria told Andrea.

"Okie doke." Andrea hopped into the truck and Gloria climbed into her car. They passed Lucy on the way as she was pulling out of her drive to head to Dot's.

The caravan of three pulled into town and parked alongside each other. The Garden Girls had officially invaded Dot's Restaurant!

Gloria stepped inside the restaurant and made a beeline for the table in the center of the room. It was the largest table inside the restaurant and usually monopolized by the "coffee clique." "Coffee Clique" was the secret name Gloria had given the group of retired men who hogged the space.

The group of men was long gone. Gloria pulled out a chair and plopped down. Andrea took the chair to Gloria's left and Lucy eased into the seat on the right.

Gloria pulled out the stack of invitations Mitzi had given her and handed Lucy the one with her name on it. Andrea had already tucked hers inside her purse.

Gloria slid the other invitations...Dot's, Ruth's and Margaret's, across the table and in front of the empty chairs.

Lucy glanced at her name scrawled on the front. "What is this?"

"A surprise," Gloria said mysteriously.

Lucy turned it over. "Can I open it?"

"Not yet. You have to wait for the rest. Then I'll explain."

Lucy rolled her eyes. "Oh no! Gloria has something up her sleeve!"

"Now what?" Dot approached the table with a tray of water glasses. She gazed at the invitations. Dot moved around the table as she set a water glass in front of each of the chairs. She reached for the envelope with her name on it.

Lucy held out a hand. "Uh-uh! You can't open it until Gloria tells us we can," she said.

Dot wiped her damp hands on the front of her apron. "I can hardly wait."

"It's a good surprise," Andrea reassured them.

"What's good?" Margaret had popped in, approached the table and pulled the scarf from around her neck. She slid into a chair, switched the card with Ruth's name and picked up her own.

Ruth was the last to make it to the party and it was well past five by the time she made an appearance. The girls were getting antsy. "What took you so long?" Dot asked.

Ruth pulled out the chair and sat. "The holidays. That's what!"

Ruth dreaded the Christmas holiday season. The workload at the post office doubled with area residents sending and receiving boxes, cards and gifts. In addition to the extra workload, she had to work every weekend, including Sundays, just to make sure everything was done.

No one was happier to see New Year's Day than Ruth!

While Ruth settled in, Dot placed a plate of goodies in the center of the table. She set six empty coffee cups on the table, along with a fresh pot of coffee. After the last Garden Girl had settled in, they turned to Gloria.

She explained how Andrea and she had met Mitzi Verona. She told them about the conversation they had, although she purposely left out the part about Kenneth, Mitzi's son. She didn't lie. She just didn't mention it.

Then she went on to say they suspected the real culprit, the person who was bribing Mitzi Verona and Commissioner Evergreen, planned to attend the party.

Lucy, the only one of the bunch who ordered hot chocolate, dumped a packet of sugar into her cup and stirred it. "Someone has the nerve to show up at the party and then take the money? Talk about gutsy!"

"Think about it," Andrea said. "There will be so many people there. It's almost the perfect crime."

The perfect crime Gloria was determined the culprit would not get away with. Not if she could help it!

Gloria waved her hand. "Go ahead...open the envelopes."

Dot, Margaret, Ruth and Lucy opened the invitations at the same time.

Lucy spoke first. "We-we're invited to the party?"

"Yep." Gloria nodded. "I'm going to catch this character and all of you are going to help!"

Gloria didn't have a plan yet. The first thing on her list was to get her hands on a layout of Mitzi's house, get a feel for the lay of the land, so to speak.

Once she had the layout, she could work on strategically placing the girls so all of the bases were covered...

"I could bring my spy equipment," Ruth offered.

It was a brilliant idea! "Why didn't I think of that?" Gloria asked. "We need a way to spy on the mailbox." She frowned. "Although it's going to be dark."

Ruth dropped the invitation in her bag. "I have the perfect tool," she said. "Leave it to me."

Somehow, Gloria believed her.

The conversation shifted to what they should wear as the girls chattered about how they had never attended a high society function.

Lucy bit her lower lip. "I'm nervous. I mean, those people are out of my league."

Gloria reached over and patted Lucy's hand. "If the guests are anything like Mitzi, you have nothing to worry about."

She smiled and told them the story of how Mitzi came barreling around the side of the barn on Sassy, her out of control horse.

"Did you get to ride horses?" Lucy loved horses. Her aunt and uncle had once owned a horse farm. When she was young, she used to beg her parents to take her to the farm to ride. The horse farm was long gone now, as were her aunt and uncle.

Gloria scrunched her nose. "No way." Gloria was the complete opposite of Lucy and deathly afraid of horses.

The girls promised to dig through their closets to try to find something to wear.

Andrea sipped her ice water. "Gloria and I stopped by the thrift stores in Green Springs and both found outfits to wear."

"No fair," Lucy pouted.

They decided if they couldn't find something in their closets, they would make a girls trip to Green Springs to see if they could scrounge up any other outfits for the rest of the group.

Gloria glanced at her watch. "I better go. It's getting late."

When Gloria got home, the first thing she did was head to her answering machine to see if Paul had called. Her heart plummeted when she saw there were no messages.

Gloria hung her coat, keys and scarf on the rack near the door. Maybe she had Paul pegged all wrong. She never would have believed he was a quitter. For him to up and take off...no warning, no notice, seemed so out of character.

Gloria wandered aimlessly around the house. She plugged the Christmas tree lights in and watched the bright lights twinkle.

Puddles stalked across the room and eyed the twinkling tree with interest. "No more chewing on the branches," Gloria scolded. Puddles had been nibbling on the fake branches and leaving little piles of green all over the house.

She finally settled in front of the computer. Mitzi Verona fascinated her. It went to show no matter who you were, no matter how much money you had, life was full of problems and complications. She thought of Percival Verona...and death.

Gloria logged on to her email. She scanned the unread messages and her heart leapt. There was a message from Paul!

"Hello Gloria. I wanted to drop you a note to tell you I am thinking of you. I tried to call the other evening but you didn't answer.

I know it seems to you I turned tail and ran but believe me, that is not the case.

I cannot tell you what I am doing right now but ask you to trust in me and know I love you with all my heart.

Soon, this whole mess will be behind us and I will be back home with my beautiful bride.

Love,

Paul"

Gloria's lower lip began to twitch. She dropped her head in her hands and began sobbing. Finally, a message that showed he still cared.

Puddles jumped onto her lap and nudged her arm. His tongue felt like sandpaper as he lapped at the tears trailing down her cheeks. Gloria snuggled her beloved cat and closed her eyes. At least now, she had something to cling to...a ray of hope.

She wiped her wet face with the back of her hand and lifted her head. Was Paul in some kind of trouble? Was this the reason he left? Maybe someone was after him, to hunt him down and he was trying to keep the person or persons away to protect his family.

Someone at the precinct knew what was going on. That someone was Paul's boss, Captain Davies.

Gloria finished reading her messages, shut off the computer and jumped out of the chair. Captain Davies was going to have an unexpected visitor. It was high time he answered a few questions!

Chapter 14

Gloria pulled Annabelle into the Montbay County Sheriff's Station and eased into a spot, smack dab in the middle of the parking lot.

She had forced herself to wait until a decent hour, 9:00 a.m., before showing up at the sheriff's station. She remembered Paul had told her Captain Davies worked the day shift and Paul would normally end his nightshift by making an appearance at the station to discuss his shift.

Gloria had no idea what Captain Davies drove or if he was even there.

She climbed the steps and made her way into the familiar lobby.

Funny how everything inside the station looked the same, but how everything was so different now, at least to Gloria.

She vaguely recognized the young officer behind the counter and glanced at her tag. Jennifer.

Jennifer smiled with a hint of recognition in her eyes. "Yes ma'am. Can I help you?"

Gloria shifted the purse on her shoulder. "I'm looking for Captain Davies."

"Your name?"

"Gloria. Gloria Rutherford." Gloria lowered her voice. "I am Paul Kennedy's fiancée."

The woman nodded. "I'll see if he's available." She disappeared behind the door and Gloria stood silently praying he would see her.

The woman returned a moment later. "Follow me."

Gloria followed her down the hall and passed Paul's office. The door was shut. She wondered if they had already moved his stuff out, boxed it up or perhaps even thrown it in the trash...

The woman stopped at the end of the hall. Gloria remembered where Captain Davies' office was located from the night Margaret and she had "cleaned" it. She also remembered how she had found a message inside the trashcan from Commissioner Evergreen.

She made a mental note to do a little more digging into the commissioner's past. After all, he was on the extortionist's hit list, too.

Captain Davies smiled and motioned Gloria into his office. He slipped out of his chair, went over to the door and closed it behind him. "Hello Gloria. I'd like to say it's a pleasure to see you but I doubt you dropped in to say hello."

"No, I didn't."

He waved to the chair in front of his desk. "Have a seat."

Gloria settled on the edge of the seat, as if at any moment she might bolt. "Paul..."

Gloria didn't know where to start, what to say and if she should even admit her suspicions. For all she knew, Captain Davies could be involved in the extortion scheme. He had opportunity.

"Why is Paul in Lansing?" she blurted out, hoping to catch the captain by surprise.

She caught a flicker in his eyes. The captain eased back in his chair, propped his elbows on the armrests and clasped his hands in front of him, his index fingers pressed against each other at the tips. "Paul is in Lansing."

Gloria wasn't sure if he was making a statement or asking a question. "Yes."

"How do you know Paul is in Lansing?" he asked.

She didn't want to throw Paul under the bus, particularly if he was on some covert operation. It was a longshot but possible. Gloria wasn't ruling anything out, or anyone for that matter.

Gloria answered his question with a question. "Did you know Paul was in Lansing?"

Captain Davies grinned. "We're going in circles, aren't we?"

Despite the circumstances, Gloria returned the smile. "Yes, it appears we are."

Gloria cut to the chase. "Are you going to charge Paul with the extortion of Mitzi Verona and Commissioner Cal Evergreen?" she demanded.

Davies narrowed his eyes and studied the woman across from him. "Now I know what Paul sees in you. You have spunk. I like that."

"Thank you."

Captain Davies leaned forward in his chair. "We are still in the midst of the investigation. Paul is...one of the suspects."

"But you have others," Gloria insisted.

Captain Davies drew a deep breath. "This investigation is a very serious matter. It involves my department and my men. Someone with inside information is bribing very important people and I have every intention of finding out who that person, or persons, is."

Gloria clutched the strap of her purse with both hands. "This involves me and my future, too, so I believe I have as much at stake as you and your department."

She abruptly stood. "Captain Davies, it appears we both have the same goal in mind. Good day." She turned on her heel and strode out of his office.

Gloria wasn't sure what she hoped to accomplish. Maybe she had hoped he would share with her that Paul was in the middle of a sting and not a suspect.

Gloria stepped out of the station and onto the sidewalk. Perhaps Captain Davies was the extortionist. Officers, especially captains, were often given unmarked police cars...with government-issued plates.

Back at the farm, Gloria settled into a chair and reached for her notepad. She studied the list of suspects...Stan Woszinski, Paul's occasional partner. Alex Tisdale, the young officer Minnie Dexter had told Gloria had been fired. Jason Endres, the other young cop who didn't like Paul.

Gloria tapped her pen on top of the notepad. She thought about Minnie, the dispatcher for Montbay Sheriff Station. Minnie knew all the ins and outs of suspects, the department and the officers. She had motive – money, but what about opportunity?

Gloria texted Officer Joe Nelson and asked him to call when he had time.

She busied herself with the final chores around the house to get ready for her houseguests. She put clean sheets on the bed in guest bedroom downstairs and then made her way upstairs to the other two bedrooms.

She rarely used the upstairs bedrooms. In fact, the last time she remembered anyone staying upstairs

was a couple years back when her sons had last
visited. If she were honest with herself, Gloria had to
admit it was too much house for one person, but the
thought of parting with it was depressing.

Her grandsons were still too young to inherit the
farm but the years were flying by and soon enough
they would finish college. She wondered if they
would want the farm then. What if they married and
their wives had no interest in living in the small Town
of Belhaven?

Gloria frowned at the thought. God had the
perfect family for the farm. She needed to be patient.

Where would she, and hopefully Paul, live after the
farms passed to the next generation? She
remembered how her sister, Liz, had enjoyed living in
a retirement community. They had oodles of
activities like golf, tennis and even bridge. None of
those interested Gloria in the least.

If she moved away, she would be leaving behind
her friends. There was always the chance she
wouldn't have to worry about it and she would be
long gone before the farm was ready to pass to the
next generation.

Gloria had threatened to move to Florida. Maybe it was time to give it some serious consideration. It would be nice to escape the cold, snowy months. Perhaps Paul and she could split their time between Michigan and a warmer clime.

Gloria finished making the beds, tidying the rooms and then headed back downstairs. She hadn't talked to her sister, Liz, in weeks and decided now would be the perfect time to give her a call.

She left Liz a message on her voice mail and started making lunch. She thawed a container of leftover turkey from Thanksgiving, pulled two slices of wheat bread from the bread bag, smeared a thick layer of mayonnaise on the bread and placed the sandwich on a paper plate.

Gloria grabbed a bag of chips from the pantry and settled in at the table. Mally and Puddles eyed her sandwich hungrily. Gloria reached inside the sandwich and pulled out a piece of turkey. She fed a smaller piece to Puddles and a larger piece to Mally.

Gloria bowed her head. "Dear Lord, thank You for this food. Thank You for my family who will be here soon. I pray they arrive safely and the weather holds.

I also ask that You help me figure out what is going on with Paul so he can come home. In Jesus name I pray, Amen."

Gloria lifted her head and stared out the kitchen window. Mitzi's party was only a couple days away. She was only a couple days away from coming face-to-face, or at least being in the same room with the person, or persons, who had turned her life upside down.

She reached inside her purse and pulled out the list of guests Mitzi had given her. Gloria slipped her reading glasses on and studied the names. Beside each of the names, Mitzi, or someone, had meticulously jotted down a brief description – hair and eye color and whom they were.

The list included the Grand Rapids' city mayor, Green Springs' mayor and several city commissioners, including Cal Evergreen.

Also on the list were local news anchors and the names of some attorneys, whose commercials she remembered watching on TV.

At the bottom of the main guest list were two smaller lists. One appeared to be Mitzi's own security detail and the other, a list of police officers who would be on hand.

Gloria didn't recognize any of the names on Mitzi's list, other than Chad Stetson, the young man Andrea and she had met the other day.

She pulled the sheet closer and peered at the officer's names. Stan Woszinski and Jason Endres. She didn't recognize the other names. At the bottom of the list was Diane Stone!

Gloria's lip twitched. Diane Stone, the female officer who had been after Paul. This would be her chance to come face-to-face with the woman who had been after her man!

Gloria saw this list as an advantage. She would get to keep an eye on them and all the while, they would have no idea who she was. Other than possibly Stan Woszinski whom she had met when she had attended Captain Davies' backyard barbeque last summer.

Gloria's home phone rang and pulled her from her deep thoughts. She scrambled out of the chair and darted over to the phone. It was her sister, Liz.

"Happy Holidays," Liz exclaimed breezily. "Let me guess. You're already sick of the nasty cold snow and are planning a visit."

Gloria walked over to the kitchen window and stared out at the snow. "Not yet but maybe after the holidays."

"How are the wedding plans going?" Liz asked.

Gloria frowned. She hadn't told Liz or even her children the wedding might be...delayed.

"Fine," she said vaguely and then quickly changed the subject. "The boys and families will be here in a couple days. I hope the weather holds until they at least make it here."

"Eric and Casey will be here tomorrow," Liz explained. "They are staying through New Year's." Eric was Gloria's nephew and Liz's only child. Casey was his soon-to-be-wife.

"How is Frances?" Gloria asked. Frances, Liz's best friend, had also moved to Florida.

"She's fine." Liz sighed dramatically. "She has a new boyfriend. Teddy something."

Gloria hoped Frances wasn't as obsessed with this "Teddy" as she had been with Milt. "Is she as crazy about Teddy as she was poor Milt?"

Liz snorted. "Heavens, no! In fact, it's the other way around. Teddy follows Frances around like a puppy."

Gloria found it hard to believe. Of course, anything was possible. "Well, I wanted to tell you Merry Christmas if I don't talk to you before then."

"Merry Christmas, to you," Liz replied. "And don't forget to email pictures of the wedding."

Liz had offered to fly to Michigan for the wedding, but with her son coming for a visit and not wanting to leave Frances alone, she decided it was best to stay put.

Gloria had promised her sister that Paul and she would visit as soon as the holidays were over and the dust settled.

The girls had planned a cruise for February. The cruise was a trip the girls had been planning for over a year now. They would be cruising with Gloria's cousin, Millie, who worked on a luxury liner. Gloria was excited to see her cousin and to take her first ever voyage on the high seas!

Gloria and her sister chatted for a few more minutes and then Liz told her she had to go. Gloria thought she heard a male voice in the background but didn't get a chance to ask Liz who the voice belonged to.

After she hung up, Gloria tossed her empty paper plate in the trash along with the napkin and headed back to the computer to finish her research on Mitzi Verona. She added Captain Davies to the list.

Her radar had gone up earlier during their visit. Gloria was convinced there was something Captain Davies wasn't telling her.

Chapter 15

Gloria placed the list of attendees face down on her small scanner / copy machine and then emailed a copy of the list to each of the girls.

Lucy was the first to call. "Wow! This is a list of the "Who's Who" in West Michigan, huh?"

"Yeah. There are some pretty powerful and public people on this list."

"People perfect for bribing," Lucy pointed out.

Gloria had the exact same thought. What if whoever was behind the extortion planned to expand their list of poor unsuspecting victims? The party would be the perfect opportunity.

"I'm nervous," Lucy admitted.

"I'm not." Gloria was on a mission...a mission to figure out who was responsible for ruining her wedding plans. Not only that, but there was a black cloud over the much-anticipated visit from her children and a damper had been placed on Christmas. It wasn't fair!

The sooner they could figure out who was blackmailing Mitzi and the commissioner, the sooner Gloria could put the pieces of her life back together.

***

Gloria shifted to the left and studied her reflection in the mirror. The party dress fit her to a "T." It would be the perfect dress to wear on the upcoming cruise with her friends. Maybe – someday – she would have a chance to show it to Paul.

Gloria pushed the thought aside. Paul was safe. He still loved her. The more she thought about it, the more she believed he was working undercover. He wasn't a suspect at all. At least that's what she had convinced herself...it was the only thing that made sense.

Gloria slipped her arms into the black bolero jacket and tugged on the bottom to smooth it out.

She glanced down at her scalloped edge, crystal encrusted pumps – her wedding shoes. She had fallen in love with them at first sight. They matched her wedding dress perfectly. They also matched the party dress.

She pointed her toe and tipped her foot. The heel was higher than what she normally wore, but they – along with the dress – made her feel like a princess.

Gloria reached for her brand-new sparkly clutch purse with the small, gold strap and strolled over to the kitchen door.

The girls had agreed to meet at 4:00 p.m. at Andrea's place to go over the details for the party. Gloria planned to place each of them throughout Mitzi's country manor. They had each thoroughly studied the list of guests and had even spent time online pulling up photographs and information on not only the suspects, but also the high profile guests who might be targets.

Ruth had been very mysterious and evasive about her spy equipment strategy, but Gloria wasn't worried. So far, Ruth had been 100% spot on with her spy equipment. Gloria was certain tonight would be no different.

Mitzi had been wonderful, giving Gloria and her friends' full access to the party planning, the list, the schedule of events, even the food.

Gloria pulled in Andrea's drive and parked off to the side. She was the last to arrive. Dot, Margaret, Lucy and Ruth were already there.

She stepped out of the car, reached across the seat, grabbed the canister that contained the poster board she had been working on and gingerly made her way to the front door. She lifted her hand to knock and the door swung open.

"Oh, Miss Gloria!" It was Alice, Andrea's former housekeeper. She clapped her hands. "You look beyoo-tiful!" she exclaimed.

Gloria hugged Alice. "Thank you, Alice," she said.

"You smell nice, too," she added before changing the subject. "The girls. They are in the kitchen."

Gloria followed Alice across the foyer, through the dining room, past the butler's pantry and into the kitchen.

The girls were dressed to the nines and admiring each other's sparkling dresses and gowns. Gloria joined the fray.

"Let me take a picture," Alice exclaimed. "In the living room in front of the fireplace." She motioned the girls across the hall, through the library and into the living room.

The girls shuffled into position with the taller girls, Andrea, Dot and Gloria in the back and Lucy, Margaret and Ruth in the front.

Alice angled the girls in different directions. When she determined she had the perfect pose, she snapped several pictures with Andrea's phone. The rest of the girls insisted on pictures as well, and Alice made sure she had all the pictures taken before letting them move.

They wandered back into the kitchen where Gloria plucked the poster from the canister and spread it out on the counter. In the center of the large white sheet was a diagram - the layout of the main level of Mitzi's country estate.

Gloria had also sketched in the horse barns, the drive, and the pool area and had drawn a large black "X" where the mailbox was located.

She had spent the entire night before, wide-awake in bed, shuffling the girls around Sunshine Estates like a chess player.

She stationed Ruth near the front of the home, close to the front yard in case she needed to keep an eye on her surveillance equipment.

Dot would hang out in the kitchen, an area she was most familiar with.

Lucy, the weapons expert, would keep an eye on the security while Andrea would stick close to the guests Gloria deemed most likely to be a targets of the extortionist, such as the mayor, wealthy business owners, etc.

Margaret would monitor Mitzi and Gloria would make her rounds.

The plan was perfect and Gloria hoped it would go off without a hitch.

Chapter 16

Ruth pulled her van off the main road and slowly made her way down the winding drive and up to the main house.

Several catering vans crowded the drive, their doors flung wide open. A beehive of workers darted back and forth from the vans to the house.

Parked next to the catering vans was another van. This one belonged to a local flower shop. The girls watched as workers carried enormous bouquets of fresh flowers indoors.

The girls followed Gloria single file into the house. Gloria heard Mitzi before she saw her. "Lordy! You can't leave it there. It has to go here! Ugh! If you want something done right, you have got to do it yourself."

Gloria rounded the corner and caught a glimpse of Mitzi tugging on a large, ornate floral arrangement. It was almost as tall as she was.

The deliveryman refused to let go and shook his head. "No. Miss Mitzi. Remember last time we placed the pièce de résistance on this table and a pint-size ruffian plowed it over?" The man tsk-tsked. "Such a mess."

Mitzi tugged back, unwilling to lose the battle. "The little monster, uh...angel, won't be here tonight, Pierre! I think we are safe."

She went on. "I will pay you double for the arrangement if you let me put it where I want," she bargained.

Pierre happy with the proposition, released his hold on the round, red drum trimmed in gold. Bursting out of the drum was a plethora of red roses, pale blue lilies and white cushion pompoms. Framing the outer edge were bright red carnations. Frilly striped ribbon bows and delicate glass glittering bulbs completed the magnificent arrangement.

Mitzi carefully carried it to the large round marble table in the center of the massive gathering room and slid it to the middle. She stood back to admire the arrangement she had designed.

Gloria made her way over to the table. "It's extraordinary."

Mitzi turned, as if surprised to see Gloria. "Thanks, Gloria. I designed it myself." She shifted sideways to look at Gloria and her eyes widened. "Well lookie here. You clean up nicely." She smiled wickedly, tilted her head to the side and kissed the air next to Gloria's face.

Now that Mitzi wasn't hidden by the enormous arrangement, Gloria got a good look at her. She was stunning in a hip-hugging, form-fitting shimmery black cocktail dress. A thick, gold braided necklace complimented the dress and Gloria would almost guarantee the necklace was the real deal.

"Ahem."

Gloria had almost forgotten about the rest of the girls, who circled 'round. Gloria quickly introduced them one-by-one, except for Andrea, whom Mitzi had met previously.

Mitzi shook each of their hands. "Wonderful," she gushed. "Thank you so much for helping me." She looked at Gloria. "Us - out."

"Thank you for inviting us." Ruth, never one to mince words blurted out. "You got quite the crib here."

Mitzi laughed. "Crib?" She looked around, as if seeing it for the first time. "Yes. I guess I do." She glanced at each of the women. "Do any of you ride horses? You should come by sometime and we can ride."

Lucy clasped her hands to her chest. "I would love to!" she gushed.

Gloria took a step back. No way was she getting on a horse. It seemed the others were taking a pass, too. Lucy, as usual, was ecstatic about the prospect.

One of the caterers approached Mitzi. "We have a small...uh, problem."

"I'll be back." Mitzi followed the caterer and the two of them disappeared inside the kitchen.

Gloria glanced at her watch. The countdown had begun. They had less than half an hour before the first guests started arriving. It was time to get a lay of the land and Mitzi had told them they had free reign to look around.

Since they were in the foyer, the girls headed up the grand staircase to the second floor where there was a hall to the left, a hall to the right and a hall straight ahead.

Gloria veered to the right and the girls went from room to room inspecting each one. It was an entire wing of bedrooms. Some had adjoining baths while others had Jack and Jill baths.

When they finished the right wing, they headed to the left. There were three more bedrooms, all with their own private bath. At the end of the hall was a double set of doors. Gloria reached for the handle and stopped. What if this was Mitzi's private suite?

Mitzi had given Gloria the green light to tour the entire house. Gloria twisted the knob and pushed the door wide open.

She gasped at her first glimpse of the room. The room was huge! It wasn't Mitzi's private quarters. It was a movie theater. A large center aisle led to the front. Covering the front wall was an enormous projection screen. On both sides of the aisle were several rows of plush, padded theater seats. There was easily room for close to a hundred guests.

Near the back and in the corner was a concession stand, complete with an enormous popcorn machine, soda fountain and snack bar.

Margaret made a beeline for the snack bar. She ran her hand along the smooth, granite top. "Wow! Check this out!"

The palatial theater made Margaret's movie room look like a lemonade stand on a street corner.

"I still like yours better," Gloria said. This one was bigger and fancier, but it didn't make it better. Without friends, it was just another room.

The others agreed. It was nice, but perhaps a tad over the top...

They stepped back into the hall and wandered to the landing. The only wing they hadn't explored was the one straight ahead.

Gloria took the lead and the girls followed behind. She had a hunch this was Mitzi's private quarters. There were two small doors...one on the right and one on the left.

Andrea opened the door on the right. It was a linen closet. The one on the left was the same.

At the end of the hall was a double set of doors, similar to the ones leading into the movie theater.

Gloria grasped the handle and turned the knob. The door was locked. "This must be Mitzi's room." She was almost relieved it wouldn't open.

The girls retraced their steps, made their way to the main level of the house and finished their tour of the formal living room, formal dining room, sitting room, library, opulent office, along with another spacious guest bedroom and bath.

They wound their way through the kitchen to the only place they hadn't been...the indoor swimming pool.

The girls found the entrance to the pool area through the back breezeway. The pool area had its own private entrance off to the side.

Gloria opened the door and stepped to the side to let the others in. She closed the door behind them and gazed at the Olympic-size pool. The pool was not square but rather rounded on both ends.

Gloria strolled over to the end. The pool was zero entry, meaning it sloped into the water instead of having a sudden drop off.

Near the front of the pool area were several luxurious lounge chairs. Tucked in one corner was a tiki bar. Torchlights stood sentinel on each side of the bar.

In the opposite corner was a wooden door with a large glass front. Gloria stepped over to the door, cupped her hands to her eyes and looked inside. "It's a sauna."

Gloria walked all the way around the pool. When she reached the back, she noticed another door. She wandered over to the door and pushed on the handle.

The door swung open and Gloria stepped inside a game room. It wasn't just any game room, but a game room Gloria's grandsons would love! There was a foosball table, air hockey, arcade machines, pinball and even a jukebox. It was every kids dream...or even every "adult" kid's dream.

"Cool man cave," Andrea said.

The grand tour had ended and if Gloria had been impressed by the sheer size and grandeur of Mitzi's "country" home before, she was now dumbfounded. She wondered how much money it would take to keep a place this size running. There would be water, electric, upkeep, not to mention taxes...or the horse farm and taking care of all those animals.

It seemed sad to Gloria the woman had tons of money and lived alone. Maybe Mitzi was content with her life. Obviously, she was. On top of that, she used her money and position for worthy causes, including the fundraiser tonight.

Still, Gloria thanked God for each of her blessings. Sometimes money could be more of a curse than a blessing. She remembered the reason she was there. Money put a target on one's back.

Gloria turned her attention to the task at hand. The countdown had begun and it was time for the girls to get into position.

Ruth slipped out of the house as she made her way down to the mailbox. She tucked a small, square device in the cover of the mailbox, closed the lid and darted out of sight.

Next, she moved the golf cart Mitzi had loaned her into position, backing it underneath a large pine tree in the corner of the yard and out of sight. She rearranged the tree branches so the surveillance camera had an unobstructed view of the mailbox.

Ruth jogged up the front lawn and onto the porch before making her way inside and over to the coat closet, although it didn't look like a coat closet. The space was more like an enormous walk-in storage closet. It was the perfect spot to set up her laptop, turn it on and tune in to keep tabs on the mailbox.

Ruth checked to make sure everything was in working order and then tracked Gloria down. It was time for Mitzi to put the envelope and the cash inside the mailbox.

Mitzi ran up to her room and returned with a small satchel. She met Gloria on the front porch. "You're sure this is going to work?" she asked nervously as she glanced around.

Gloria shook her head. "No. I'm not sure it will work. It may not work, but what other options do we have?"

Mitzi frowned. "True."

Gloria tapped the top of the satchel. "You didn't..." She had instructed Mitzi not to put $255,000 inside the envelope. She had convinced her to put $2,500 inside and if the culprit wasn't caught, she could tell the person the note she received said $2,500, not $255k. She wasn't sure if that strategy would work, or if it would enrage the extortionist.

Mitzi had placed a one hundred dollar bill on the top, another one on the bottom and a bunch of ones in the middle of the banded packs.

Gloria waited at the top of the drive while Mitzi drove down to the end, shoved the money in the mailbox and closed the front. She drove back up the drive and parked her Range Rover in front of one of the garage doors.

"It's time to get this show on the road." Gloria linked arms with Mitzi and the women stepped into the house to wait for the guests.

Chapter 17

The place went from empty to full in a matter of minutes. Mitzi stood near the entrance shaking hands and kissing the air for what seemed like forever.

Gloria stepped to the side and kept one eye on Mitzi and the other eye on the door. The line had no end.

Certain everything was going as planned she made the rounds, checking on Margaret, Andrea, Ruth in the closet, Dot in the kitchen and Lucy who was keeping a watchful eye on security.

Everyone was raring to go and the party kicked up a notch and into full swing.

Uniformed butlers circled the main level of the house with silver trays full of exquisite hors d'oeuvres while other butlers made the rounds with trays full of flutes of expensive champagne.

In addition to the free flowing champagne, there was an open bar in the foyer and another in the library.

Mitzi knew how to throw a party and all of the guests seemed to be enjoying themselves. Of course, practice made perfect.

Front and center, next to the beautiful floral centerpiece Mitzi and the florist had battled over, was a silent auction event. On the other side of the table was a donation box, shaped like Santa's sleigh where guests could slip their cash donations inside.

Not only was there the silent auction and donation box, each guest had paid $100 to attend the fundraiser.

The silent auction offered a variety of items including a couples' massage, dinner at upscale restaurants, tickets to the theater. There was even an auction for a new golf cart with a year's membership to Green Springs Country Club thrown in.

Gloria worked the crowd. It was a shame the guests weren't wearing nametags. It was tricky for Gloria to figure out who the list of possible targets might be. Mitzi had explained she no longer used nametags since the pins and fasteners tended to damage the clothing of attendees.

Not only that, but also this event was more intimate than most and Mitzi knew all of the guests, which didn't help Gloria one iota.

Of course, most of Gloria's suspects worked security. She wandered over to Lucy. "How is it going?"

Lucy nodded. "Good. I've picked up on all your suspects including Jason Endres, the Stone woman and Stan Wosz...Wosz."

"Woszinski," Gloria said.

"Yep. Him."

"Any suspicious activity?"

"Nope." Lucy shook her head.

Gloria patted her arm. "Keep your eyes peeled."

She wandered into the kitchen to check on Dot, who was taste testing a canapé. The petite treat was a towering mound of cheese spread with what looked like a sprig of arugula on top.

Dot popped it into her mouth. "This is so good," she moaned. "Here, try one." She handed the bite-size morsel to Gloria who nibbled on the edge. It was delicious. It sure didn't taste like the pasteurized cheese spread Gloria was familiar with.

"See anything unusual?" Gloria asked.

Dot's eyes darted around the room. "Oh!" Her eyes grew wide. "There was this one guest who came out here raising a ruckus. Something about peanut allergies and he almost ate something with nuts."

She rolled her eyes. "He seemed like a real jerk."

Dot tugged on Gloria's sleeve. "Hey! There he is!"

A tall man, wearing a black and white tuxedo strolled out of the kitchen, down the steps and out the back door. "I think he smokes," Dot guessed.

That would be Gloria's guess, too. Now that Gloria thought about it, Dot had a perfect view of the back door and could easily keep an eye on who went out and came back in. "Anyone else?"

Dot nodded. "Yeah. There have been a few. A few of the cops on your list, the guy I just pointed out, along with a couple women."

"Keep up the good work."

Gloria wondered if Ruth had a hit yet. She wandered out of the kitchen, past the throngs of guests to the makeshift surveillance room in the front. She tapped on the closet door and it opened a crack.

"It's me. Gloria," she whispered. The door swung open, Gloria slipped inside and closed the door behind her.

"See anything yet?"

The glow from Ruth's computer screen was the only light in the small space. Ruth studied the monitor. "Nope. Not yet. Seen a few cars stop at the end of the drive but nobody got out."

Gloria eased onto her knees and scooched close to Ruth. "How does it work?

"Well, I put a small motion activated device in the door of the mailbox. When someone opens the door, a small alarm sounds. Not in the mailbox mind you, but on here." She pointed to the computer.

"Once the alarm sounds, I flip on the infrared camera attached to the front of the golf cart hidden under the large pine tree near the mailbox. The camera will capture a picture of the person, clear as a bell, as if it were the middle of the afternoon." Ruth snapped her fingers. "Voila! We've got 'em."

Gloria glanced at Ruth's outfit. She was wearing a black pantsuit and...white sneakers. "Ruth!" She pointed to the shoes.

"What? I can't run in heels," Ruth argued.

Gloria had never seen Ruth wear heels...or a dress for that matter.

Gloria grinned. She pushed herself to a standing position and patted Ruth on the shoulder. "I'm sure you'll catch something on that camera. I have faith in you," she said before she stepped out of the closet and quietly closed the door behind her.

She passed Margaret in the living room on her way to track Andrea down.

Andrea was in the corner, trapped by a middle-aged couple. She gave Gloria a look that screamed for help. Gloria made her way over.

"There you are." Andrea reached for Gloria's hand. "I was telling Commissioner *Evergreen* and his wife, Beverly, we are planning a cruise early next year."

Gloria lifted a brow. City Commissioner Cal Evergreen. The same man Dot pointed out who kept going outside. Gloria leaned in. She could smell the lingering scent of cigarette smoke on his jacket.

Gloria held out a hand. "Pleasure." She wasn't sure if it was a pleasure or not.

He gazed at her with steely eyes. "You look vaguely familiar."

Gloria forced a smile. "I hear that all the time."

"Beverly! There you are!" A woman wearing a black and white ballroom gown approached.

The commissioner's wife disappeared to chat with another guest. Evergreen lingered. He honed in on Andrea and glanced down at her ring hand. "What is a beautiful woman like you doing at a party like this...all alone?"

Gloria shifted. It was as if she were in visible. "She's not alone," Gloria sniffed.

Evergreen gave Gloria a hard look, grabbed Andrea's hand and raised it to his lips. "The pleasure was all mine."

He dropped her hand and walked away.

Andrea waited until he was across the room before she turned her hand over. In it was a card. "He gave me his card." She flipped the card over. On the other side, someone had scrawled a phone number.

Gloria tugged on a strand of stray hair and glanced at Evergreen. "Snake." She remembered Evergreen had been caught with a prostitute. Maybe he deserved to pay a little money, feel a little pain. "Have you heard anything else?"

Andrea shook her head. "Nope. No one looks suspicious."

The look of disappointment on her face caused Gloria to smile. The smile quickly faded. She hoped this night wouldn't be a complete waste of time.

Gloria glanced at her watch. The party ended at 10:30 and it was already half past nine. The culprit would have to make his move soon.

She turned to go when Ruth burst out of the closet, swung the front door wide open and disappeared from sight.

Gloria was hot on her heels with Andrea right behind her.

Chapter 18

Bright floodlights illuminated the front yard. Gloria raced across the manicured lawn as fast as her heels would allow.

Andrea, a little more accustomed to the heels, pulled away from Gloria and quickly gained on Ruth. She lifted the hem of her skirt to reveal a gun holster strapped to her upper thigh.

Still running, Andrea pulled the gun from the holster and picked up the pace.

Ruth and Andrea reached the mailbox just as a dark sedan squealed out of the drive and roared off down the road.

Andrea lifted her gun and fired off several rounds. She lowered the gun. "He got away but I think I hit the car." At least she hoped she hit the car.

Gloria came to a screeching halt next to them. "Was it a patrol car? What did it look like?" she gasped.

Ruth frowned. "It was too dark to tell. I don't think it was a patrol car."

Gloria glanced back at the house. Whoever took the bait was now gone.

"Lucy!" Gloria shouted. Lucy was still inside, keeping tabs on the suspects.

Gloria tugged one shoe off and then the other. She lifted the hem of her dress and full out ran across the cold, hard lawn toward the house. When she got to the porch, she dropped her shoes on the cement floor and shoved her feet in the shoes.

She sucked in a deep breath, smoothed her skirt, ran her fingers through her hair and stepped back inside.

On the outside, she was cool as a cucumber. On the inside, her heart was pounding, her mind racing and her attention focused on one thing...figuring out who had left the party.

Lucy was right where Gloria had left her, completely unaware of the events that had just taken place.

Gloria casually sidled up next to her. "Anyone missing?"

Lucy scanned the guards. She stepped outside to take a headcount. Lucy knew exactly who was working security. No one had gotten past her. No one.

She stepped back inside the room and sauntered over to Gloria. "Nope. All are accounted for."

Gloria's heart sank. Her eyes met Lucy's. "Are you positive?"

"Let me check again."

Gloria waited...and prayed Lucy would come back with a different answer this time.

"Nope. Still all here."

Gloria's shoulders drooped. She was certain one of the officers had been involved. After all, who else could have planted the money and notes in Paul's locker? It *had* to be someone who had access to the locker room!

Gloria shuffled into the foyer where most of the guests had gathered. Andrea casually strolled over. "Well?"

"All of the suspects have been accounted for. We're back to square one."

Andrea's eyes scanned the room. "Maybe not." Andrea turned to face the wall. She reached inside her bra and pulled out the business card she had tucked away...the card City Commissioner Cal Evergreen had given her.

She flicked her wrist and held the card out. "Where did he go?"

Gloria eyes darted around the room. Evergreen was nowhere in sight. His wife was still there. She was off to one side, talking to one of the nightly news anchors...a young man with dark hair and a fake smile. "He's probably out smoking."

Gloria headed outdoors. She crossed the porch, wandered around the yard, circled around the garage and stepped back inside.

She remembered Dot was keeping track of who was going outside and who was coming back in.

Dot's back was to her as she faced the kitchen sink.

Gloria tapped her shoulder.

Dot swung around. She was wearing an apron.

Gloria stuck her hand on her hip. "Dot Jenkins! What are you doing?"

Dot wiped her wet hands on the front of the apron. "I can't help myself. Plus I was bored."

She untied the apron and placed it on the counter. "But I've been keeping tabs on who all has gone out and come back in." She pointed to the large window in front of the sink.

The glass window was like a mirror and Gloria watched as a guest – a woman – stepped outside.

Gloria lowered her voice. "Remember the jerk who went on about the nuts...Commissioner Evergreen?"

Dot's eyes widened. "That was Commissioner Evergreen? Yeah, he's outside."

It dawned on Dot where Gloria was headed. "You think *he* might be the one?"

It was exactly what Gloria thought. "I have a brilliant idea."

She looked around the room. "Where's Andrea?"

Gloria tracked down her young friend and explained her plan.

Andrea scrunched her brow. "You think this will work?"

If City Commissioner Cal Evergreen was the snake Gloria now suspected he was, she was almost 100% certain her plan would work. "Go ahead and make the call."

Andrea nodded, reached for her handbag and headed to a quiet corner to call Evergreen to set up a rendezvous.

Andrea dialed the number on the card. The conversation was brief. After she finished, she pressed the "end call" button, shoved the phone in her bag and made her way over to Gloria. "Forty-five minutes."

Gloria nodded. "That should be plenty of time." The place quickly cleared and the next time Gloria looked at the clock, it was ten thirty. Mitzi gave instructions to the cleaning crew and met the girls in the living room.

Mitzi lowered her voice and looked around. "How did the sting go? Did we get a hit on the money?"

"Sort of," Gloria hedged. "We've got 'em...him...on the run. Now all we need to do is nail him down."

"Is there anything I can do to help?" Mitzi wanted to nab this person as much as Gloria did.

Gloria shook her head. "We think it's Commissioner Evergreen."

Mitzi's hand flew to her throat. She touched the thick gold necklace with the tips of her fingers. "Oh my!"

"But...but I heard he was part of the extortion, too. Someone found out about him and some..." Mitzi waved a hand in the air. "...escort service."

"Unless it was a cover," Andrea theorized. "That would certainly throw police off."

"There is one puzzling thing." It was something that had just occurred to Gloria. "If Evergreen took the money and ran, he left his wife behind."

Mitzi shook her head. "Good heavens. Those two never go anywhere together. Why I heard they don't even live in the same house anymore. The marriage is a sham and for appearance sake only so Cal can keep winning elections."

Still, there was another accomplice. Someone inside the police department. Gloria remembered the other night when she had taken out the trash and noticed a police cruiser parked next to a government-issued vehicle.

Gloria stood abruptly. "We have half this case cracked. Now to figure out the rest."

The girls climbed into the van, but not before promising Mitzi that they would let her know as soon as they were able to name the suspects.

***

Earlier, Gloria had had to hurry and make a decision on where to have Andrea meet Evergreen. She could think of no better place than home turf...Belhaven.

The girls dropped Andrea off at home so she could pick up her truck. Before she got into her truck, Ruth hooked a tiny mic to the back of Andrea's dress so they could listen in on the conversation.

Ruth followed Andrea's vehicle into town and then backed the van into the dark alley next to the post office before she shut off the lights.

She placed the monitor on top of the dashboard and pressed the button. "Andrea, do you copy."

Static.

"Yep. Loud and clear."

Gloria's main objective was to figure out if there were bullet holes in the back of Evergreen's vehicle. The thought ticked Gloria off. The scumbag frequented houses of ill repute, all the while living off taxpayer's dollars. He was probably paying for it with her money!

On top of that, the man had nearly ruined Gloria's life. Well, maybe not ruined but made it pretty darn miserable!

A light illuminated the back of Andrea's parked truck.

"Someone is coming," Ruth hissed.

Dot, Lucy and Margaret leaned forward and five sets of eyes focused on Andrea's truck. A dark, four-door sedan pulled next to her.

The girls watched as Andrea slid out of her truck and approached the back of the car. "Good girl," Gloria whispered. "Check for bullet holes."

Andrea casually leaned against the back of the car and ran her hand along the trunk as Cal Evergreen edged closer to Andrea.

It was a game. He moved closer. Andrea moved away.

"If he so much as touches Andrea, I'll march over there and punch his lights out," Gloria vowed.

Andrea placed her purse in front of her, using it as a barrier to keep Evergreen at bay.

Gloria could have sworn she saw Andrea tilt her head and nod. It was Andrea's signal she had found what she was looking for.

"Let's roll!" Ruth reached for the driver's side handle. Gloria reached for the passenger door handle.

They flung the doors open and hopped onto the pavement.

At the same time they hit the ground, Gloria heard the sound of tires squealing. Headlights bounced wildly off the front of the restaurant.

Gloria blinked. In an instant, cop cars surrounded Andrea and City Commissioner Cal Evergreen. Not one or two cop cars, but a parade of cop cars.

The doors of the cop cars swung open and uniformed officers poured out of the vehicles, guns drawn. "Hands up!"

Andrea and Evergreen raised their hands in the air.

A couple officers shoved Evergreen to the ground while another pushed Andrea forward so both her hands pressed flat against the trunk of the commissioner's car.

"Oh my gosh!" Gloria had a horrifying thought. "You don't think police think she's a ..."

"Streetwalker!" Four women shouted simultaneously.

"Stop! Stop! You have it all wrong!" Gloria raced across the parking lot and darted across the street.

One of the officers, a very familiar officer, turned. "Gloria?"

Gloria came to a screeching halt. "Paul?"

"What…"

Andrea glanced over at Paul, who was holding her wrist, getting ready to handcuff her. "Hi Paul."

"Andrea?" Paul lowered the cuff and faced Gloria. "Someone has a lot of explaining to do."

Gloria crossed her arms and raised her voice. "You got that right!"

Chapter 19

Andrea left her truck parked in front of Dot's Restaurant and climbed into Ruth's van for the ride to Montbay County Sheriff's Station.

Andrea slipped into the middle seat, smack dab between Margaret and Dot. She shuddered as she reached for her seatbelt. "They almost arrested me."

Margaret patted her hand. "Welcome to the club, dear."

Andrea thought about what she had just said. Margaret and Gloria had been arrested. Lucy, Ruth and Dot had been taken to the police station for questioning. So far, Andrea had been the only one to dodge the bullet.

The girls proceeded to argue as to whether the brief event constituted a full-blown incident.

Dot and Margaret thought it should count since Andrea was scared half to death. Lucy, Ruth and Gloria disagreed since Paul was the one who was going to arrest her and he didn't count. Now if it had been an officer they didn't know...it might have counted.

"That's a technicality," Andrea argued. "I was taking the fall!"

"True," Gloria agreed. "Okay. We'll give it to you."

Gloria's mind wandered to Paul. He had a lot of explaining to do. She went from being relieved, to being hurt. At that precise moment, she was downright livid.

By the time Ruth pulled the van into the police parking lot, she had cooled off. The least she could do was give him a chance to explain.

Captain Davies was waiting for the girls in the lobby. He motioned them to the back and they followed him into the cafeteria / conference room.

Gloria winked at Margaret as they stepped inside. Hopefully the girls hadn't been busted.

Captain Davies sat at the end of the table. Paul sat next to him. Gloria took the seat directly across from her betrothed. She wanted to study his face as he explained what had gone down.

Dot, the mediator, sat next to Paul, to protect him in case Gloria went after him. She doubted it, but then Gloria had been under extreme duress. Anything was possible.

The rest of the girls settled into their seats and turned to face Captain Davies.

He ran a hand through his cropped gray locks and scratched the five o'clock shadow on his chin. "I'm going to guess you ladies were on to Commissioner Evergreen."

Margaret nodded. "Andrea shot the back of his car," she said.

Davies raised a brow. "Which one of you is Andrea?"

Andrea raised her hand. "Me," she answered in a small voice.

Ruth was in her element. She loved the thrill of the chase. The fact they got their guy gave her a huge adrenaline rush. "I caught him on camera."

Davies turned to Ruth. "Camera?"

She nodded. "Yeah. We set up surveillance at the party. When he went for the money inside the mailbox, we went in for the kill. So to speak," she added.

"Money in the mailbox?" Davies was clearly confused.

Not Paul. This was just the beginning. There was a whole story behind it and he knew beyond a shadow of doubt that his beloved bride-to-be was right in the thick of it. "So you set up a sting to flush out the extortionist."

"To clear your name," Lucy added as she looked at Paul.

He turned his gaze to the woman seated directly across from him. "What are friends for?"

"We volunteered," Dot said.

Captain Davies turned to Paul and chuckled. "Man, you weren't kidding when you said she was a handful."

Gloria decided it was time to turn the tables. "So. I'm guessing Paul is no longer on leave and no longer under suspicion."

Davies nodded. "Paul agreed to help flush out the mole here in the department. It looks as if we were working one end of the investigation while you fine ladies were working on the other end."

Gloria had no intention of airing her dirty laundry and gave Paul a look that told him in no uncertain terms they would have a nice long chat later. "Who was the mole?"

Six sets of eyes turned to Captain Davies. "Diane Stone. She enlisted the help of her corrupt buddy, Evergreen. They hatched a plot to set Paul up. In the meantime, they collected tidy sums of cash from Mrs. Verona."

"But how..."

"How did Stone get into the men's locker room?" Davies shrugged. "The same way you two snuck in there, posing as cleaning people."

Gloria glanced at Margaret and lowered her gaze. Busted.

He went on. "Paul caught Evergreen in the prostitution ring. Evergreen and Stone joined forces where they schemed to defraud Mrs. Verona.

Evergreen made it look like he himself had been a victim to throw us off."

"I saw a patrol car and government vehicle out back the other night...so I'm guessing that was Diane Stone and Commissioner Evergreen?" Gloria asked.

Paul raised a brow. "It probably was."

Gloria had one final question. "Why travel to Lansing?"

Paul grinned. "I was doing a little research on Commissioner Evergreen. That's when we started to focus our investigation on him."

"How did you know where to find him tonight?" Margaret asked.

Captain Davies placed his elbows on the table and leaned forward. "We had a sting set up for him tonight and when our inside guy noticed him hand a card to a beautiful, blonde lady dressed to the nines, they followed him to Belhaven."

Andrea blushed. "Do I look like a..."

Paul patted her hand. "You are a lovely young woman, Andrea. You hit the detective's radar, that's all."

The women exited the cafeteria and stepped into the hall. Captain Davies held the door and then followed Paul out. "We'll get your retirement party in the works."

He turned to Gloria. "Paul has agreed to stay on part-time and work special assignments. Undercover when we need him."

Gloria shifted her purse and peered at Paul. "He has, has he?"

Paul put his arm around Gloria's shoulder. "No different than what you do, my love. The only difference is I'll get paid for it," he joked.

Lucy laughed. "He's got you there, Gloria."

Davies extended his hand, took Paul's in a warm grip and patted him on the shoulder. "I guess I'll be seeing you at the wedding." He winked and turned to kiss Gloria's cheek. "I can't wait to see this beautiful bride."

Outside on the front steps, Paul turned to Gloria. "Am I in the dog house or can I drive my lovely bride-to-be home?"

"You better drive her home," Ruth warned. The girls each hugged Gloria and made their way over to Ruth's van.

Paul opened the door of the unmarked police car and waited for Gloria to settle into the passenger seat. "By the way, have I told you today how absolutely ravishing you look?" he asked.

Gloria grinned as she reached for her seatbelt. "Flattery will get you everywhere," she warned.

Chapter 20

Gloria smoothed the front of the dress with a trembling hand. She tugged on a stray strand of hair that had fallen in her eyes. "You don't think the dress looks too tight?" she fretted.

"Nope! You are the most beautiful bride I have ever laid eyes on," Lucy assured her.

Ariel, Gloria's granddaughter, slipped her hand inside her grandmother's hand. "You look like an angel," she said, her bright green eyes gazing up in adoration.

Gloria knelt down and wrapped her arms around her only granddaughter. "Why thank you, Ariel. You look like an angel, too. The prettiest angel in the whole wide world."

Three towheads burst through the doorway and hopped over to Gloria. It was her grandsons Oliver, Tyler and Ryan, dressed in miniature three-piece suits. Her ushers. "Grams. Everyone is waiting!" Ryan said.

Right on cue, the organ music drifted into the room.

Lucy, Dot, Margaret, Ruth and Andrea circled their friend while Gloria's four precious grandchildren tucked in between and they bowed their heads.

"Dear Heavenly Father, we thank You that Gloria *finally* made it to the altar. We thank You for this beautiful day where we can share in the joy of these two lives joined together and we pray for many years of wedded bliss," Dot prayed.

"Amen," the girls agreed.

"Ay-men!" Ollie shouted enthusiastically.

"Walk the girls to their seats," Gloria instructed her grandsons. The boys each dutifully grabbed the girls' hands and led Gloria's closest friends to their seats.

The place was jam packed with over one hundred of Gloria and Paul's closest friends and neighbors...the entire Town of Belhaven.

When the others disappeared, Ariel turned to Gloria. "Ready Grams?"

Gloria sucked in a deep breath and closed her eyes. "Yes, Ariel. I'm as ready as I'll ever be."

Ariel picked up her basket of flower petals and led her grandmother out of the library, down the hall and across the foyer.

Ariel sashayed down the red runner, dropping rose petals as she made her way to the front.

Gloria stepped through the French doors and into the festively decorated room. Her eyes were immediately drawn to the man standing at the front. Not Pastor Nate, but the other one. The love of Gloria's life.

His eyes met hers and the corners crinkled as he smiled at his bride.

Gloria's heart fluttered and she tightened her grip on the bouquet of flowers she was holding.

Eddie and Ben, Gloria's sons, stepped forward. Eddie tucked his arm through his mother's right arm while Ben slipped his arm through her left. The trio began a slow stroll down the red carpet.

Ariel twirled around, the petticoats of her frilly satin dress dancing in the air. She stopped near the front, next to her brother, Oliver, and her cousins, Ryan and Tyler.

Gloria tried to pace herself as she moved forward in a slow, steady stroll. She turned her head and smiled at the guests, all of the faces so near and dear to her.

Gloria's daughter, Jill, her husband, Greg, along with Eddie's wife, Karen, and Ben's wife, Kelly, looked on.

Jill gave her mom the thumbs up.

Across the aisle, on the other side, were Paul's children, Jeff, his wife, Tina, and his daughter, Allie. They smiled at Gloria, happy that their father had finally found someone...the right one.

Ariel, impatient for her grandmother to pick up the pace, motioned her to hurry, which made the guests closest to the front chuckle.

In the row, seated directly behind Gloria's children, were Dot, Ray, Margaret, Don, Lucy, Max, Ruth and Slick Steve or just, Steve, and Andrea and Brian. Last, but not least, was Alice, who winked at Gloria when she caught her eye.

When Gloria reached the front, Paul stepped to the side and gazed at his bride with adoration.

Gloria bent down, hugged Tyler, Ryan, Ollie and Ariel. She released her hold and the children scampered off to sit next to their mothers.

Eddie leaned forward, kissed his mother's cheek, shook Paul's hand and quietly made his way over to sit next to his wife.

Ben was next. He kissed his mother's cheek, wrapped his arms around her in a warm embrace and then turned to Paul. "She's all yours. Good luck."

The crowd chuckled and Paul grinned. "I can't wait!"

Paul and Gloria solemnly turned to face Pastor Nate. "Well, there were several of us here who wondered if this day would ever come."

For the second time, the guests started to laugh and Gloria frowned.

Paul he reached over and squeezed Gloria's hand.

"Dearly beloved guests..."

The ceremony went off without a hitch and when Pastor Nate told Paul he could kiss his bride, Paul wrapped his arms around Gloria's waist, pulled her close to him and kissed her passionately. He was reluctant to let go until the wolf whistles from the guests echoed in the room.

Gloria giggled and lifted a hand to her flushed cheeks.

"Get a room!" a good-natured guest shouted.

"We did," Paul informed them with a chuckle. Paul tilted Gloria upright and grabbed her hand.

"Ladies and gentleman, I am thrilled, beyond measure, to present to you Mr. and Mrs. Paul Kennedy."

Applause erupted. Everyone jumped to their feet and clapped as Paul, holding tight to his bride's hand, walked down the aisle.

The two of them waited on the other side of the doors as the guests and well-wishers, one by one hugged the newlyweds.

The last ones to exit the room were the Garden Girls. "It was perfect," Lucy gushed.

"One of the most beautiful weddings I've ever been to," Dot agreed.

Margaret patted Andrea's hand. "Andrea, you outdid yourself."

"Thanks," she said. "But I couldn't have done it without Alice."

"Of course," Ruth said. "Alice is like a speed demon, zipping around doing this and handling that."

Alice smiled. "Thank you."

"Thank *you*," Gloria smiled and hugged Alice.

Alice tugged on her skirt. "I must go check on the food."

Dot nodded. "I'm right behind you."

Dot and Alice had joined forces to whip up some tempting dishes for the reception. Although Gloria and Paul had paid for the food, Alice and Dot had insisted on putting everything together. It was their gift to Paul and Gloria.

There were standing rib roast, mounds of fried chicken, crockpots full of meatballs, baked and mashed potatoes, fluffy rice, corn, green beans, and dinner rolls, not to mention scrumptious, bite size desserts.

To top it all off there was the wedding cake. Gloria decided on a simple sheet cake. Half the cake was white and the other half chocolate.

While the guests lingered in the foyer sipping champagne and toasting the newlywed couple, workers quickly brought in round tables, covered them with white linen tablecloths and then placed the chairs around the tables.

Several tall, twinkling trees dotted the perimeter of the room and when Andrea dimmed the lights in the sunroom, the sparkling lights cast a romantic glow.

The guests feasted on the scrumptious goodies.

It was a festive event and a celebration that no resident of Belhaven would soon forget.

When they finished eating, the army of workers cleared the tables.

"Attention everyone!" Andrea clapped her hands and the crowd quieted. "It's time for Gloria to toss the bouquet."

Several of the single women clustered together in the front of the room. Eleanor Whittaker, Sally Keane, Bea, Gloria's hairdresser. Lucy was there, too, along with Andrea. Ruth didn't make a move as she sat in her chair and crossed her arms.

"C'mon Ruth," Lucy urged.

"Nope." Ruth shook her head and stubbornly refused to budge.

Gloria marched over, grabbed her hand and dragged her into the crowd.

Satisfied everyone was in place; Gloria turned her back to them, kissed the tip of the flowers and tossed the bouquet over her head.

Sally dove for it, Lucy jumped to catch it. Despite their attempts to catch the bouquet, it landed squarely in Andrea's hands. She gazed down at the bouquet and turned to Brian.

Gloria grinned. Brian had purchased an engagement ring for Andrea, but he had told Gloria he didn't want to steal her thunder so he decided to wait. Brian planned to propose to Andrea on New Year's Eve.

Brian smiled and shoved his hands in his pockets. Andrea scurried over and showed him the bouquet.

Brian leaned over and kissed her forehead. "Guess we're next," he teased. He winked at Gloria.

Gloria couldn't wait until he popped the question. Several times, she had almost slipped but caught herself. She would never forgive herself if she ruined Brian's big day.

It was time to cut the cake and Paul led his bride to the cake table. He sliced a piece of white cake and a slice of chocolate cake. They lifted the cake and waited for the pictures before gently placing the cake in the other's mouth.

Music drifted from the sunroom and Paul and Gloria headed back inside for the first dance. Gloria stepped into her husband's arms and they slowly circled the dancefloor, lost in the moment. So perfect...so right.

Gloria blinked back the sudden tears and Paul caught a glimpse.

"Oh no. You're not regretting it already," he teased.

Gloria let out a shaky laugh. "No. It is just so perfect."

Paul lowered his head and tenderly kissed Gloria's lips. "God has truly blessed us."

The song ended and the DJ Gloria and Paul had hired began playing a song for the mother/son, father/daughter dance.

All of Paul and Gloria's children...and grandchildren swept out onto the floor and one by one danced with the bride and groom.

After the dances, the DJ picked up the tempo and the younger guests hit the floor.

Gloria and Paul made their rounds, talking to guests, thanking them for coming.

They had specifically requested no gifts; but rather, asked that they donate to Gloria's new pet project, literally. "At Your Service."

Marco and Alice told Gloria earlier in the day they had close to a thousand dollars donated in their name and Gloria was thrilled.

The magical evening finally wound down and Gloria and Paul said farewell to the last guest. The only ones left were the Garden Girls. Even Paul and

Gloria's children had headed out with sleepy grandkids in tow.

"When are you leaving for your honeymoon?" Brian asked.

Paul draped an arm around Gloria's shoulders. "Tomorrow afternoon. Tonight we are staying in a five star hotel in downtown Grand Rapids," he explained.

Gloria had left the honeymoon planning to Paul and he had been very mysterious about where exactly they were going. It was a complete surprise.

"Have a wonderful honeymoon and *try* to stay out of trouble," Margaret teased.

Paul shook his head. "No telling what will happen on this trip," he groaned.

Gloria hugged her dear friends and then followed her husband to his pick-up truck.

The drive to Grand Rapids gave the two of them a chance to wind down and chat about how magical the day had been.

Paul had reserved a suite, complete with champagne, red roses and Belgium chocolates. He dropped Gloria off near the entrance and drove off to find a parking spot.

They quickly checked in and with room key and overnight bag in hand, headed to their room, located on the seventh floor. When they stepped into the elevator, Gloria gave Paul a quick glance. The night she had been waiting for, thinking about was finally here. The thought made her heart flutter.

The palms of her hands began to sweat and she wiped them on the front of her dress.

Paul, noting her nervousness, reached for her hand. "Nervous?"

Gloria wrinkled her brow. "Kind of," she admitted.

Paul tenderly swept the back of his hand across her cheek. "I promise. I don't bite, although I might nibble a little."

Gloria smiled. "Are you sure?"

The elevator doors opened, they stepped into the hall and walked to their room.

He stopped abruptly in front of the door. "This is it," he announced.

Paul slipped the key card in the door. When the door opened, he dropped the overnight case inside the door and stepped back out. In one swift move, he swept his bride into his arms and carried her across the threshold, the door closing behind them.

Moments later, the door popped back open and Paul placed the "Do Not Disturb" sign on the outside of the door.

The end.

The series continues. Look for Garden Girls Book #11, coming soon!

About The Author

Hope Callaghan is an author who loves to write Christian books, especially Christian Mystery and Cozy Mystery books. Born and raised in a small town in West Michigan, she now lives in Florida with her husband.

She is the proud mother of one daughter and a stepdaughter and stepson. When she's not doing the thing she loves best - writing books - she enjoys cooking, traveling and reading books.

Hope loves to connect with her readers!

Visit **hopecallaghan.com** for information on special offers and soon-to-be-released books!

Email: hope@hopecallaghan.com

Facebook: www.facebook.com/hopecallaghanauthor

Other Books by Author, Hope Callaghan:

DECEPTION CHRISTIAN MYSTERY SERIES:
Waves of Deception: Book 1 - **FREE**
Winds of Deception: Book 2
Tides of Deception: Book 3
Samantha Rite Series Box Set - Books 1-3

GARDEN GIRLS CHRISTIAN COZY MYSTERIES SERIES:
Who Murdered Mr. Malone? Book 1 – **FREE!**
Grandkids Gone Wild: Book 2
Smoky Mountain Mystery: Book 3
Death by Dumplings: Book 4
Eye Spy: Book 5

Magnolia Mansion Mysteries: Book 6
Missing Milt: Book 7
Bully in the 'Burbs: Book 8
Fall Girl: Book 9
Home for the Holidays: Book 10
Garden Girls Christian Cozy Mysteries Boxed Set Books 1-3

CRUISE SHIP CHRISTIAN COZY MYSTERIES SERIES:
Starboard Secrets: Book 1
Portside Peril: Book 2
Lethal Lobster: Book 3
Deadly Deception: Book 4
Book 5 – COMING JANUARY, 2016!

SWEET SOUTHERN SLEUTHS (Short Stories):
Teepees and Trailer Parks Book 1 – **FREE!**
Bag of Bones Book 2
Southern Stalker Book 3
Two Settle the Score Book 4
Sweet Southern Sleuths Box Set: Books 1-4

FREE Books and More!

Visit my website for free books, new releases and special offers: **hopecallaghan.com**

If you enjoyed reading "Home for the Holidays", please take a moment to leave a review. It would be greatly appreciated! Thank you!

Grandma Louise's Best Ever Christmas (Sugar) Cookies

<u>Cookies – Ingredients List #1</u>:
2-1/2 cups flour
1 cup white sugar
¼ tsp. salt
1 tsp. baking soda
2 tsp. cream of tartar

*Mix dry ingredients in large bowl

<u>Cookies – Ingredients List #2</u>:
1 cup butter, softened
2 eggs
1 tsp. vanilla

*Mix wet ingredients

<u>Directions</u>:
Preheat oven to 350 degrees
Mix both wet and dry ingredients together. (You can also refrigerate dough so it "firms up.")
Roll cookie dough on floured surface. Cut with cookie cutters.
Place cookies on ungreased cookie sheet.
Bake for 6 – 10 minutes (depending on thickness)
*You can add more flour if the mixture seems "doughy"

Frosting
½ cup solid vegetable shortening
½ cup softened butter (not melted)
1 tsp. vanilla
4 cups powdered sugar

2 tbsp. milk
food coloring

Cream butter & shortening
Add vanilla
Slowly add sugar
Add milk
Beat on high until fluffy. (This recipe will test your mixer. I recommend using a heavy-duty mixer, but it is not required. Just keep an eye on the mixer so it doesn't overheat.)

*You can also add a little extra milk, a tablespoon at a time.
Separate frosting into bowls. Add drops of food coloring until color desired is achieved.
Frost cooled cookies. Decorate with sprinkles, etc.